Tutti Frutti

Written and Illustrated by

JOHN · BYRNE

BBC BOOKS

To Little Richard

Tutti Frutti Cast list

Danny McGlone Robbie Coltrane
Suzi Kettles Emma Thompson
Eddie Clockerty Richard Wilson
Vincent Diver Maurice Roeves
Bomba MacAteer Stuart McGugan
Fud O'Donnell Jake D'Arcy
Dennis Sproul Ron Donachie
Janice Toner Katy Murphy
Glenna McFadden Fiona Chalmers
Noreen Diver Anne Kidd
Sheena Fisher Annie Bruce
Stuart Inverrarity David Dixon
DJ at Radio Buckie John McGlynn
Blond Young Woman Louise Beattie
Sister in Kilmarnock Ginni Barlow

Photographs © BBC and BBC Enterprises Ltd
(Nigel Robertson)

Published by BBC Books
A division of BBC Enterprises Limited
35 Marylebone High Street, London W1M 4AA

First published 1987

ISBN 0 563 20547 4

Typeset in 10/11pt Sabon by
Ace Filmsetting, Frome, Somerset
and printed in England by Redwood Burn, Wiltshire

Suzi

Danny

Vincent

Dennis

Bomba

Fud

Eddie

Janice

Noreen

Glenna

The Boy Can't Help It!

The Co-operative hearse crawled up the hill towards the newly reopened lair that had been the McGlone family's last resting place since 1958. Eddie Clockerty, his cropped iron-filings hairdo covered by a film of dew, stepped onto the gravel and waved the vehicle down. As the Majestics' manager for the past twenty-five years, who better to supervise the transfer of Big Jazza's remains from the hearse to the grave? The three surviving Majestics – Vincent Diver, a Jack Palance lookalike running to seed, Francis O'Donnell, ferret-faced and known to their legions of fans as Fud, and Bomba MacAteer, the cherubic over-the-hill drummer – all dressed in black and wearing Ray-bans, broke reverentially into their own *a cappella* version of the Cochran classic, 'Three Steps to Heaven'. It was a heartbreaking sound.

The elderly priest opened his missal and began intoning the De Profundis. The grieving widow, Theresa, dolled up to the nines, fought her way to the front of the cortege and, with the help of daughters Doreen and Brenda-Lee, placed a hand on the coffin as it was manhandled across the damp grass.

There was a loud sniff. All eyes turned to Dennis the roadie, standing beside the Majestics' battered Transit van some forty yards away. He had forsaken his Levis for a suit. It was hired, and a far from perfect fit.

Next came the floral tributes. The first, from 'Miss Toner & All at Manhattan Casuals with Deepest Sympathy', was in fuchsia pink. Following it came a nine-foot-long Fender Stratocaster in pale cream chrysanths, with 'Jazza McGlone 1940-86' picked out in blood-red rosebuds and 'Rock 'n' Roll Will Never Die' the full length of the fingerboard in forget-me-nots – a touching farewell to a colleague who, in the finest traditions of the business, had been crushed beyond recognition in an automobile smash. . . .

At least, Danny thought so. Danny McGlone was the deceased's younger brother by some ten years, and as such had felt obliged to hotfoot it across from New York the minute he got Eddie Clockerty's cable. He'd gone there six and a half years before to try and sell his paintings, but when Eddie's wire arrived he was working a South Bronx toilet playing non-stop Billy Joel for ninety bucks a week.

The news of Big Jazza's sudden death had come as a blessing in disguise – except that Clockerty had only sent him enough to cover his air fare one-way. All he had in the world was the powder blue suit with the pegged pants he stood up in, plus what he'd managed to cram into the Macy's bag he was clutching, incongruously, at the graveside.

The last handful of earth rattled off the coffin lid. Dennis the roadie stepped into the circle of mourners, one of Big Jazza's stage suits draped over his arm. A nod from Theresa and three hundred quid's worth of primrose shantung floated down into the inky blackness and arranged itself into a grotesque parody of the Big Guy's busted frame.

Big Jazza

The priest slammed his missal shut, Eddie grabbed Theresa's arm, and Vincent Diver signed a couple of autographs for the gravediggers. It was all over. Danny felt sick. Not quite as sick as when Big Jazza had flushed his tortoise down the toilet on the morning of his seventh birthday, but pretty sick nevertheless. Brenda-Lee slipped a thin wad of bills into his fist and instructed him to 'Look after the ground staff'. By the time he'd done that the limos had beat it and he was left alone with Dennis and the Transit. Danny made a silent vow never to attend another funeral as long as he lived. Dennis took him by the sleeve and led him towards the van.

'Twenty-five years in rock 'n' roll on the fifteenth of next month, and your stupid brother has to go and get himself totalled,' he moaned as they swung out of the cemetery. 'You realise we're goin' to have to cancel the Silver Jubilee Tour now, don't you?' Dennis lit a cigarette and squeezed the Transit between the bus and the oncoming bin lorry with his knees. He asked Danny where he wanted to be dropped off.

'I thought we were goin' back to Theresa's?'

The roadie's cheekbones tightened. 'No, no ... *they're* goin' back to Theresa's.'

By 'they' Danny took it he meant Diver, O'Donnell and MacAteer. 'Sufferin' God, he was *my* brother,' Danny burst out. 'I can surely go back to his place for a drink after his funeral?'

The question was plainly rhetorical, but that wasn't how Dennis took it. 'There's three outfits where blood ties don't count for *that* much, Danny Boy.' His stubby thumb and forefinger snapped out the emphasis. 'The Magic Circle, the Mafia and the Majestics.'

Danny felt his head swim. The nausea he'd been fighting back at the graveside suddenly overwhelmed him. He groped for the window-winder, found it, wound down the window and deposited his in-flight egg'n'waffle breakfast on the passing pavement. He fell back into his seat and wiped his face with his sleeve. The crummy, roach-infested one-room walk-up he shared with the Funny Shoe Salesman on 42nd Street was calling him back. He remembered all the things he hated about Glasgow. One of them was the Majestics' roadie. The rest were the Majestics and Eddie Clockerty.

'Where d'you say you wanted me to drop you off?' The roadie enquired, oblivious to Danny's recent manifestation of grief.

What the hell, thought Danny disgustedly, he needed that drink.

⭐

Dennis crashed the lights and pulled the Transit to a protesting halt outside what looked like a Mexican cantina on the corner of the wide and windy street. Danny climbed stiffly out of the van and staggered to the kerb, wondering where all the manky Glasgow dives he'd ever been chucked out of had vanished to. The Transit lurched off into the streaming traffic with Dennis's hand on the horn. Danny, undaunted, pressed his shades onto his nose and gave the stained-glass door of the cantina a dunt.

It was dark inside, but not so dark that he couldn't make out the unmistakable bulk of Big Jazza coming towards him out of the gloom, wearing a powder blue suit with pegged pants and swinging a Macy's bag in his left mitt. Of all the dumb locations to stick a seven-foot mirror, he thought, cursing to himself. He hadn't realised till that moment just how much he'd grown to look like the Big Guy.

He climbed the stairs to the first level and found a table next to a Joshua tree. He didn't know it then, but what had started out as possibly The Worst Day of His Life So Far Without Exception was about to turn itself on its beanie and become The Worst Day of His Life So Far Without Exception With One Exception.

The One Exception came sashaying from behind a clump of cactus and asked for his order in a South Side accent. Danny gave her the once-over and nodded his head in approval. She had short hair the colour of Keiller's Thick Cut Marmalade all combed up on top, and a way of looking at a guy with those smoky-green orbs that made him forget all about Lauren Bacall but not about how to pucker up and whistle. There was something about the way she spoke that rang a bell with Danny, but he was damned if he could put a name to her. ...

'Danny? Danny McGlone? What are you doing here?'

She had the advantage of him. Danny racked his jet-lagged brain but couldn't come up with the red-haired vision's handle.

'It's me, Suzi. Suzi Kettles.'

Danny lowered the shades. The name was the same, but the Suzi Kettles he remembered from Glasgow School of Art twelve years back could only be described as a dog. He ordered a Martini. If this doll was a dog, he was Orphan Annie.

She asked him how was New York. He'd forgotten how small the Glasgow art world was. *Everybody* knew your business.

He told her New York was just terrific and that he was just across for his brother.

She enquired how his brother was getting on. Was he still playing with that band? You didn't hear much of them nowadays. What was it they called themselves again?

'The Majestics. No, he's jacked it in.'

She said that was a shame, but if they weren't getting anywhere in the charts that was the wisest course. 'Did they not play at an Art School hop one time? They weren't all that hot, were they?' She made a rueful face.

Danny didn't feel like discussing the Majestics right at that moment.

'I remember you had on these green trousers. They were hilarious.' She threw back her ginger coif and showed off her teeth.

Bloody hell, he thought, that was all he needed . . . a doll with perfect munchers and total recall.

When she recovered, she asked him if he wanted an olive in his Tequila Sunrise.

He reminded her he'd asked for a Martini. Very dry.

She told him they were foosty, which Danny found difficult to believe. Martinis didn't go foosty, did they?

'The olives, stupid.'

He told her, thanks for letting him know.

She said, don't mention, and went to get his order.

Danny took off the shades and rubbed his fists into his dampening eyes – which, he told himself, possibly explained how come he didn't happen to catch precisely what she muttered to herself while she was waiting for the bar-hop to fix the Martini. It *sounded* like, 'God, Danny McGlone . . . what an ugly-lookin' big guy!'

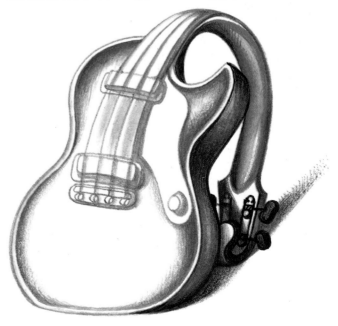

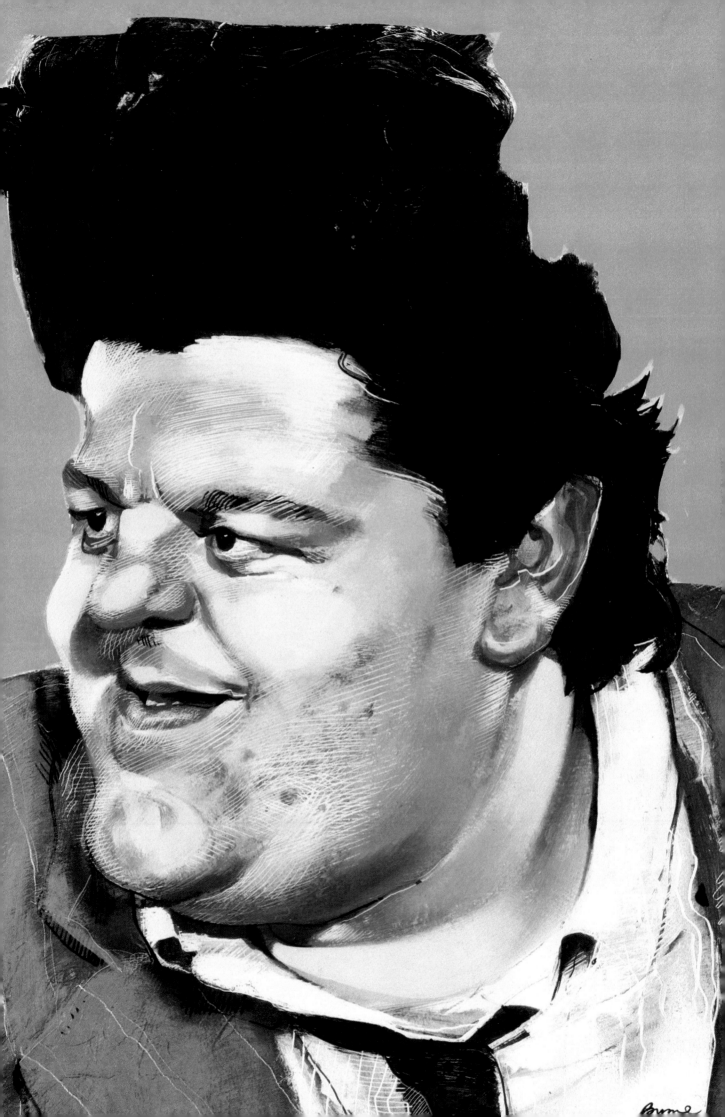

The more senior of the two VAT men had been scrutinising the photograph on the wall of the Clockerty Enterprises office in Cambridge Street for a good forty minutes. It showed Eddie Clockerty embracing Frank Sinatra outside the Sands Hotel in Las Vegas, but one would have needed a magnifier to detect the skilful paste-up joins.

The younger VAT man cleared his calculator display. There had been one or two minor discrepancies in the accounts, but nothing too exciting. Another bum tip-off. 'Did I hear you mention another set of books, Miss . . . er?' It was always worth a try.

'Toner.' Janice broke off filing her nails and swung her legs onto the floor. 'D'you want me to get them for you?' She squeaked her way round the desk to the fridge. The PVC two-piece was the appropriate colour for this solemn day, but noisy. A generous application of black lip salve completed the mourning outfit. Janice passed the contents of the fridge across the desk and wondered who had tipped them off.

The young man came across an invoice for 'Six Dozen Pairs Frankie Avalon Loafers (all left feet)' in the first of the school exercise books, and fed the figures into his calculator.

'I was up all Tuesday night cryin' my eyes out.' Janice bit off a ragged chunk of pinky nail and spat it decorously into the waste-paper basket.

The VAT man looked up and smiled briefly, then returned his attention to the calculator.

'I mean, how'm I supposed to get into my work now?' Janice pocketed the nail file. 'It was Mr Clockerty's motor the big eejit wrote off when he ran into the bus shelter. Who's goin' to pick us up in the mornin's? He doesnae expect me to fork out bus fares on what he pays me.'

The glimmer in the VAT man's eye had been replaced by the steely glint of the harpoonist preparing to land a big one.

Janice held her nails up to the light. 'D'you both take milk in your coffees?'

'You're a funny guy, McGlone.'

Why, he wondered. Because he liked Martinis and had a predilection for medieval petit point? He took Suzi's arm and steered her through into Twelfth Century Tapestries, his favourite room in the entire Burrell Collection.

'I'd be upset if *my* only brother had just got himself killed.'

Ah, she was that kind of a doll, thought Danny comfortingly.

But while appreciating her concern, it was his sister-in-law he was feeling sorry for. The Carpet Discount Showroom in Shawlands would have to go. Not to mention the bungalow in Cambuslang.

When Suzi asked if his brother's insurance wouldn't cover all that, Danny just guffawed. The only thing Big Jazza ever had insured was his Fender Strat, he told her, and as far as he knew the band still had that.

'What about this manager, then? Wasn't it his car?'

'We're talkin' about Eddie Clockerty, sweetheart.'

She obviously hadn't come across Eddie's type, mused Danny, otherwise she wouldn't have suggested Theresa taking him to court. Yeah, that was a good one. The post mortem had shown the Big Guy was nearly six times over the limit, and all Eddie had had to say was he'd taken the car without asking. Anyhow, he thought, pulling himself together, he hadn't brought Kettles out here to discuss Big Jazza's dependants' problems – it was *his* problems that concerned him. The first of which was his amnesia.

'Are you absolutely positive you're the same Suzi Kettles – the horse-faced doll me and Jimbo Abernethy used to pap putty rubbers at in Life Drawing? What happened?'

Some dolls just don't know how to accept a compliment, he thought as Suzi responded with exaggerated sarcasm. What did she want him to tell her, that he'd always thought she was a boy? Because he had. Danny urged her to pack a bag and come back with him to New York.

'So you *are* going back?'

What kind of a stupid question was that? Of course he was going back. He had a highly promising painting career to pursue, hadn't he?

'Yeah, Abernethy was saying.' She strolled through into Oriental Ceramics.

The pangs of jealousy clawed at his stomach lining. Abernethy? When had she seen Abernethy? Danny caught up with her and casually enquired what the hell she thought she was playing at consorting with that crud?

She denied 'consorting' with anybody – the guy was a regular at the cantina, that was all. Him and his cronies from TV.

TV? Like a repair shop, did she mean?

'No, like a TV producer, stupid.'

The last time Danny had seen Abernethy, he recalled, the arse was hanging out of his sanshoes. Not any more, apparently. He was now into aftershave and the kind of canvas suits that French peasants fling on their compost heaps when they're done with them. Danny invited her again to come to New York, told her he'd dump Laurie Anderson and maybe even get her on the cover of *Women's Wear Daily*.

No dice. It turned out she'd had a two-year stint as a stewardess flying transatlantic twice a week out of Prestwick after she graduated from Drawing and Painting, and if she never saw New York in her life again it would be way too soon. Before that she'd had an unfulfilling four-year stretch trying to teach art to unappreciative scruff who were more interested in fondling the female form than in immortalising it in poster paint.

He was finding it more and more difficult to believe that this was the same doll that had been nuts about him all through Art School. According to Abernethy, that was.

He put his hand in his coat pocket. Three crumpled dollar bills and forty-seven cents in loose change.

'Let's go eat, Monkey Face,' Danny suggested in his best Cary Grantese. So you blow three, four bucks on a chick, he thought, what's the big deal?

★

Eddie ran an eye over the racks of 'Authentic US Menswear' and groaned. American fifties' clobber might be what all the kids were clamouring for, but few of those kids were actually beating a path to the door of his emporium. The entire Manhattan Casuals stock would hardly fetch two grand, never mind seven, which was what he'd worked out he owed in VAT.

Janice's voice floated down to the shop from the upstairs office. 'That's your beef tea out, Mr Clockerty.'

Eddie thought of Wee Tommy Cairns, his co-producer from Carntyne Promotions, and the months of work they'd both put in on planning the Silver Jubilee Tour ... the souvenir programmes, the T-shirts, the projected double album of *Majestics' Greatest Hits* ... all down the swanee, and all because of that nincompoop, Big Jazza. Nothing for the VAT man there. ...

The voice called again, more stridently now. 'If you don't get a move on this beef tea's goin' down the sink!'

Eddie made his way shakily up the stairs and tried to think who might have it in for him, who it was that had tipped off the Customs and Excise. Too many names sprang too immediately to mind.

'There's four Oxo cubes in that, so don't go slooterin' it down your shirt front.' Janice placed the steaming mug of grey-brown liquid on Eddie's desk and crossed to her corner of the dingy office. 'How'd the funeral go? Big turnout, was there?' She blew the dust off the typewriter keys and made a face into her make-up mirror. The unaccustomed exercise had brought a disagreeable flush to her chalk-white cheeks. It didn't go at all well with the black lip gloss.

Eddie loosened his black crocheted tie and raised the mug to his lips. As if she gave a monkey's how the funeral had gone.

'Shame about the Silver Jubilee Tour, eh? Still, you cannae very well have a band goin' out on the road fronted by a stiff, can you?'

'No, but you can have the next best thing, Miss Toner,' Eddie said, snapping out of the doldrums. He picked up the phone and dialled the Carntyne Promotions number.

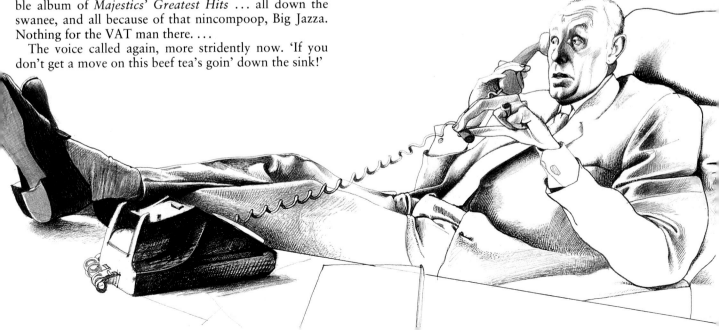

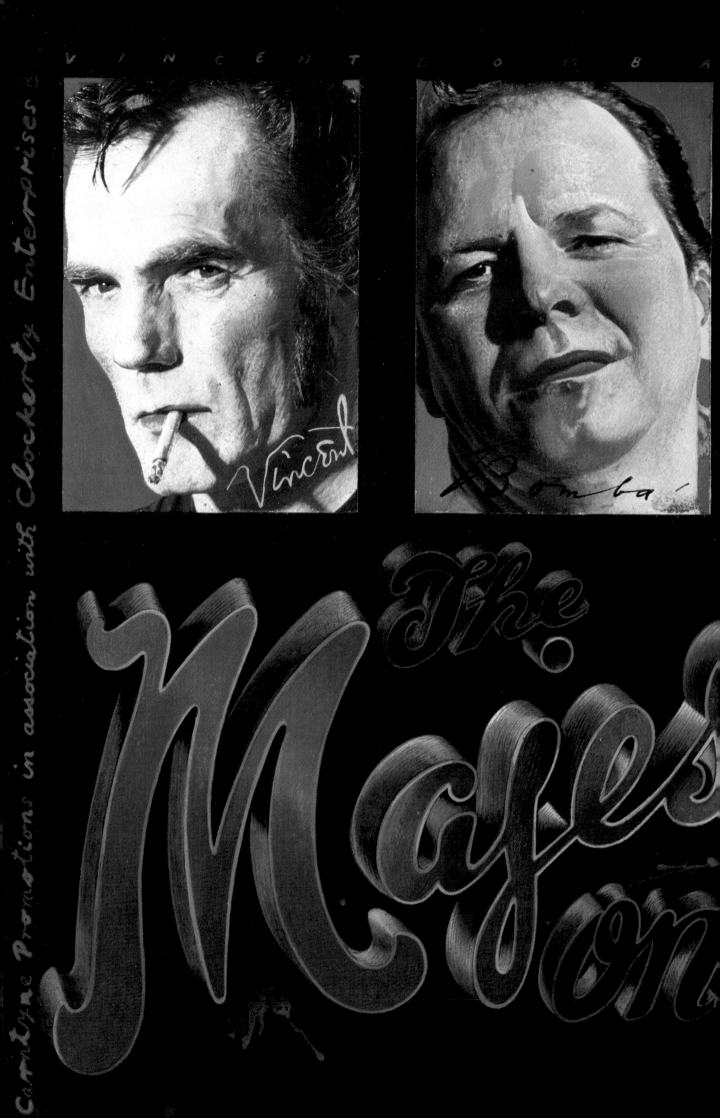

'Two houses, Fud.' Bomba shook his head in dismay. 'Even Elvis never had *two* houses.' He removed his shoes, as per Vincent's instructions, and placed them on the mantelpiece beside the framed snapshot of Glenna. This post-funeral invite was the first opportunity the drummer and the bass guitarist had had to cast a jaundiced eye over what Diver called his Other House. Bomba picked up the photograph of Glenna and regarded it with distaste. She was even younger-looking than he'd been led to believe. The pinched features plastered with make-up and the sawn-off miniskirt served only to underline the waif-like qualities that Vincent seemed to find so alluring. Bomba's top lip curled. He had a daughter of twelve who looked more mature.

'I didnae realise we'd be visitin' a mosque,' said Fud, running the soles of his socks over the new cream tufted carpet. He tried to guess how much of a discount Jazza had given Vincent and his newly acquired, not to mention obsessively houseproud, mistress.

Dennis wobbled round the door with a trayload of coffee mugs. Vincent appeared at his back, a whisky bottle in one hand, a pile of drink mats in the other. He watched the roadie like a hawk as he put the tray down on the glass-topped table. One spot on that new carpet and there would be ructions.

'You were sayin', Vinnie?' Bomba was anxious to pick up the conversation where they'd left off at Theresa's, and then get back home ... the twins were teething and his elderly mother was babysitting. But it was a conversation he knew they had to have.

'All I'm sayin' is, supposin' we came up with somebody a bit younger, that was all.' Vincent poured a generous measure of whisky into his coffee mug and rubbed one stocking sole over the other. His nostrils twitched as the acrid fug of sweaty sock mingled with new carpet smell in the room.

'Younger than Springsteen, you mean?' Bomba put the question warily. Since the night of the accident they'd been through every possible candidate for lead singer over the agreed age limit.

'Bit younger than that even.' Vincent took a swig of fortified Nescafé and wondered to himself if he dared risk opening a window.

Dennis got to his feet. He'd heard quite enough of this conversation. He had a good idea of what was coming next. 'I'll be outside in the wagon, you guys.' He padded across to the door.

'Hold on, I'll get your footwear.' Vincent reached for the door handle.

'Let him get his own bloody footwear.' Bomba knocked his cigarette ash into one of Fud's shoes and sank back into the sofa. 'Carry on, Vinnie.' Bomba watched the lead guitarist closely.

'Are you not supposed to have some kinda underlay with this garbage?' Fud O'Donnell ... one wife, seven weans, no mistresses ... was wont to dwell more on domestic matters than on the exigencies of the band.

'We *are* talkin' about a *guy*, I take it?' Bomba flipped his drink mat across the room. His voice was flinty.

Vincent grabbed the whisky bottle by the neck and swayed across to the mantelpiece. He put the bottle down next to Glenna's picture and ran a finger round the frame.

That clinched it. Any lingering doubts in Bomba's brain were now resolved. He jerked a thumb at Fud. 'C'mon, you! Grab your bootees ... we're leavin'.'

By the time Vincent had caught up with them, the bass player and the drummer were halfway up the drive towards the Transit.

Vincent hung on to the gate and harangued them. 'She might only look about fourteen, but I'm tellin' you ... this chick could blow King Kong off the stage when she gets worked up!'

The drummer's response as he climbed aboard the wagon was terse. 'Let's go, Dennis.' The Transit pulled away from the kerb.

'Ask yourselves ...' Vincent's voice rose to a whine ... 'would I try and land us with a bummer?'

But the Transit was already rounding the corner of the tree-lined avenue.

The Majestics' guitar ace slammed the gate and stomped back down the drive. He banged his fist on the front door and punched his way along the hall. 'Stupid pigs!' Vincent shouldered his way into the lounge and barged across to the window. Twenty-five years, and when it came to the crunch they didn't trust his judgement. He turned to the half-empty whisky bottle on the mantelpiece.

It was a full nine seconds before the trail of mucky footprints traversing the virgin cream of the carpet fully registered. Aw, Christ. ... He looked down at his manky, mud-covered socks. *Aw, Christ!*

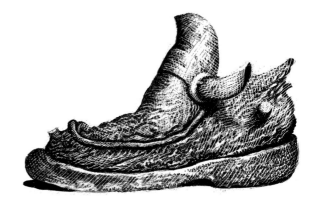

Dennis stared at Eddie in disbelief. 'What d'you mean, *find him*? He could be halfway back to New York by now.'

Eddie crabbed round the roadie and took the pair of peg-bottoms the customer was holding.

'Tell you what I'll do, son.' He laid the discoloured trousers on the counter. 'Since there does appear to be a slight bruising of the fabric just under the crotch here, I'll let them go for thirty-five, how's that?' He switched off the smile and turned to Dennis. 'Tell him it's a benefit gig for his sister-in-law.'

Dennis stubbed out his cigarette on the heel of his cowboy boot and stuck it behind his ear. 'I don't think Vincent's goin' to be too happy with this arrangement.' He crossed to the door.

'Bugger Vincent!' Eddie selected the largest pair of kiddies' ankle socks from the box marked 'Assorted Argylls' and chucked them onto the counter. 'Compliments of Manhattan Casuals, there you go.'

Dennis was standing at the open door. 'Did you say a benefit gig?'

'Prior to the Silver Jubilee Tour, aye.'

Dennis stood to one side while the customer slipped into the street.

'You don't want me to discuss dough with Danny Boy, do you?'

Eddie looked stunned.

Dennis shrugged. He pulled the door behind him as he left for the cantina.

★

'Remind me never to order Chicken Harry Lauder in a Greek taverna ever again.'

Danny could hear Suzi rummaging through her kitchen cabinet looking for the Alka-Seltzers they both needed – same went for him re the Sea Bass Armenian Style, he thought nervously, rolling his hanky into a ball and wedging it in his gub.

'You never said where you were staying in Glasgow, McGlone,' she called.

Nor did he intend to. Not till he was safely tucked up in bed beside her. Danny took a look around the apartment … the Charles Eames chair, the Bush portable radio, the great pile of *Horizons*, the Dansette record player all testified to a doll with taste, he reckoned. What separated Kettles from the millions of other such dolls was the collection of 78s sitting on the bookshelf. Eve Boswell's 'Pickin' a Chicken', Alma Cogan's 'Bell Bottom Blues', Dickie Valentine's 'Finger of Suspicion' … not only did he feel he was about to be seduced by an aesthete, but one that could sing all the words to Nervous Norviss's 'Apecall'.

Danny stuck Guy Mitchell's 'Singin' the Blues' on the Dansette and unplugged his tonsils … he and Guy rolled happily into the verse.

Suzi came bouncing out of the kitchen and plucked the arm off the record. 'I'll get your jacket.'

Danny sat up on the sofa in mock amazement. What did he want his jacket for, he asked her. He could sing perfectly well in his shirtsleeves.

As Suzi flung the said jacket at him her voice was shaky. 'Not only do I fork out twenty-odd quid for a possible dose of botulism, but I'm expected to provide a bed into the bargain! You're not on, McGlone.' She crossed to the door and held it open.

Danny explained that all he wanted was a bit of shuteye and that he'd be quite happy to curl up on the sofa.

'You've got one minute to beat it, McGlone.'

He offered to curl up on the carpet.

'One minute, then I start screaming.'

He confessed to an old football injury – she was perfectly safe. …

'Fifty-six seconds. …'

It was her hormones, right? He had hormones as well, he pleaded, only they weren't working at the moment – there was nothing to worry about.

'Fifty-four, fifty-three. …'

That wasn't going to work, clearly. Danny slipped his coat on and walked to the door. He was now so weary that his torso felt cut off from his undercarriage. Suzi let go the door and made a bolt for the bedroom, still counting. Trust me to pick a fruitcake, he thought angrily. …

Suzi meanwhile sat cross-legged on the bed, her eyes riveted on the alarm clock. 'Seventeen, sixteen, fift …' She heard the front door slam.

The clock tick-tocked the silence away. Suzi got up and crept across the room. She took hold of the door handle. A tiny squeak made her jump. She inched open the bedroom door and put an eye to the crack. Not a sound. She waited. All she could hear was the clock. She tiptoed the few feet to the front door and threw the snib. Her heart was pounding. She turned and leaned her back against the door.

'*Waaaaaaaaaaaaaaaaah!*'

There he was. He'd never left. She could have kicked herself, falling for such a sucker punch.

★

The dawn chorus of coughing pigeons brought Danny round. He tried easing his cramped withers into a more comfortable hollow in the tub, but only succeeded in getting his freezing legs snarled up in the threadbare quilt. Sufferin' God, this was only supposed to happen in movies – the icy water from the dripping tap ran down his big toe, along the back of his calf and up his thigh.

Suzi swept into the bathroom and ordered him up. 'Get a move on, McGlone. This chap'll be here in a minute.'

Aha, so there *was* a 'chap' after all! That was a relief, thought Danny. He had the reputation, albeit self-endowed, of being irresistible to women. He wrapped the quilt round his middle and followed her into the living room.

'So you've got a chap, have you?' he said, mimicking her South Side accent. He chuckled to show there was no ill feeling.

She shoved a bowl of Weetabix into his hand. 'Your road manager, I'm talking about. Don't use all the milk.'

Road manager? That was news to Danny. He didn't know he had a road manager.

She told him he was just off the phone, and would he please stop giving her phone number to every two-bit jerk in the country. 'Take a good look around you, McGlone. What d'you see?'

'A very pleasant apartment. I'm glad I live here.'

'Like hell you do!'

He was taken aback at the sheer narkiness of her tone.

'What you see is one of everything. *One* chair, *one* cup, *one* plate. And you know why you only see one of everything?'

He wasn't all that good at conundrums, he knew, especially in the wake of a particularly bumpy transatlantic flight, a harrowing funeral, a Greek bot-blaster and seven sleepless hours in a strange bathtub, but that was an easy one. 'You're skint, right?' he sympathised.

'Because I live alone, by myself, nobody else, just me, because that's how I like it!' she corrected.

At last they seemed to be getting to the nub of this curious monomania. There had been a chap. One chap, or more than one?

The doorbell went. So did Suzi, straight into the shower. Danny forced another Weetabix between his teeth and went to answer the door. Yes, he thought, they say it's difficult to get that fifth Weetabix over, and they're right. Especially when you see who's outside on the landing.

What the hell did Dennis want?

★

'He never went and signed it, did he?' Janice's eyes widened in astonishment as she placed a cup and saucer on the blotter. 'That's yours with the lumpy milk.'

Eddie opened the right-hand desk drawer and took out a sheaf of papers covered in densely packed type.

'Of course he signed it, Miss Toner.' He carefully fitted one of the sheets from the drawer on top of the single page that constituted the contract between Danny McGlone and Clockerty Enterprises, and began painstakingly tracing Danny's signature. 'He just didn't sign *all* of it.'

Janice leaned over his shoulder. 'You could go to prison for that, Mr Clockerty.'

'For correcting a clerical blunder?' Eddie's eyebrows arched. 'Surely not, Miss Toner.' He went on with his delicate task.

When the telephone rang Janice answered it. 'Good afternoon, Clockerty Enterprises.' She listened, then held out the receiver. 'Vincent Diver. He doesnae sound too pleased about somethin'.'

Eddie concentrated hard on getting the loop on the G just right. 'Tell him I'm away home, Janice.'

'You've just told him.' Janice dropped the phone onto the counterfeit contract.

Eddie picked it up and placed a hand over the mouthpiece. 'You are on a verbal warning, m'girl.'

'Aye, that'll be right,' she retorted, giving him one of her looks.

Eddie cleared his throat and put on his 'What-can-I-do-for-you-old-son?' voice. 'Vincent, what can I do for you, old son?'

Janice slid Eddie's cup across the desk towards him. 'You better drink this before it congeals.'

Glenna scraped the last little bit of vinyl trim from the Cortina's steering wheel and sighed. She put her head back, stared at the yellowing roof and wondered if the guy in the cowboy boots and the dumb features had given Vincent her message about where to find her. The bark of a stray dog crossing the litter-blown car park brought her out of her reverie. She stared across the bleak stretch of concrete to the low building with its graffiti-scarred walls and couldn't think why, if the Majestics were all that Vincent cracked them up to be, they had chosen such a scabby, isolated dump for their lead singer's widow's benefit gig. Especially in this, their ... what was it again? ... their Golden Jubilee Year?

'Talk about fickle?' Suddenly Vincent appeared and thrust his head inside the window. 'I thought you told me last night it was better if we didnae see each other unless it was absolutely ....' He looked at Glenna's face. 'Aw no ... don't tell me.'

'I'm afraid so, honey. I went to see the doctor this morning and it's for definite.' Glenna chewed her lip and tried to look upset.

Vincent lurched away from the car as if he'd just been kneed in the groin. 'Aw, Glenna ....'

The advertising signs on the outside of the decaying lounge bar flickered into life, rendering the scene even more depressing. The stray dog loped up, sniffed at Vincent's jeans, then cocked its leg.

★

'That first set was murder, pal.'

Danny hardly needed the drummer telling him that, but he grimly smiled his thanks and squeezed past to get to his rented keyboards. What in God's name, he wondered, had possessed him to imagine it was going to be anything like *The Girl Can't Help It*? He thought back to the three days' rehearsals out at Bomba's place ... the fall-outs, the fights, the insults ... and fingered the swelling under his right eye. He'd get Diver for that.

The setting for the gig did nothing to uplift the spirits either. The Bon Accord Social Club, Shotts. Now, there *was* a misnomer. There was nothing 'social' or even sociable about the joint. What looked like a thick-pile carpet on the floor between the tables was in actuality the build-up of fag ends, vermin and capsized chicken suppers sluiced down with upset lager and ground into the linoleum. The furnishings were your basic Festival of Britain 'moderne' tarted up with household enamel, and what passed for a stage backdrop had seen better days adorning the town's Christmas tree ... *circa* 1947, possibly. Oh, yeah – and the toilets had another six months to go before their annual hose-out.

Danny knew he was dying on that stage. They all were. And it was all his fault. Suzi had warned him it wasn't going to work ... he should've listened to her. Thank God she wasn't here now to witness his humiliation. It wasn't difficult to work out how much Theresa was going to benefit from this gig. The Bon Accord patrons, all seated in serried ranks and all of them with their backs turned to the stage, were definitely not going to be digging deep into their Terylene flares and plastic bucket bags to give generously to a band they'd just booed off in the first half. Theresa would be lucky if she got enough for an unsliced loaf from this bunch of zombies.

'Danny?'

Besides feeling nauseated he must also be hallucinating. If he didn't know that Suzi had no intention of coming....

'Danny?'

Even viewed the wrong way up from between his legs

she still looked sensational. Danny rammed the piano jack into the amp and straightened up....

'Kettles!'

With singing heart Danny watched her park herself next to the miserable-looking Munchkin – as he'd christened Glenna – who Diver had been deep in conversation with during the interval, and flash her molars at him. The muse came down from the blistered ceiling and settled happily on his shoulders. He felt a fire kindle in his crepes and burn up into his belly....

'Have I missed much?'

Danny shot her a look. His fingers crashed onto the keys and the opening bars of 'Tutti Frutti' came thundering out of the speakers.

'You ain't heard nothin' yet, kiddo!'

Diver's jaw dropped open in amazement as he strapped himself into his Gretsch. Eddie slittered his tomato juice all over his mohair jacket. Even Fud was caught on the hop. The piano rolled and Bomba picked up the beat. Vincent leaped onstage and chucked a few choice licks into the mix. Fud's Rickenbacker thumped into action and pinned the whole damn thing to the wall. It felt good being in love, Danny congratulated himself, and it sure as hell felt good being a Majestic.

'Waaaaaaaooooooooooooooooohhhhhhhh!!!!'

On the Road Again

The orangey-gold glow from the street lamp outside her bedroom window formed a perfect halo around Suzi's head as they lay there in the dark. For the first time Danny noticed that her nose had a little bump in it. The only other nose he'd seen like that was on an angel in a Fra Angelico *Annunciation*. She turned her face to his.

'Who the hell's Glenna?'

He reminded her of the benefit gig a couple of weeks back.

'Aw, yeah, the smout sitting next to me that ordered Bacardi and Babycham, right.'

He was with some difficulty trying to persuade Suzi to accompany him on the first leg of the Silver Jubilee Tour, due to kick off first thing in the morning, and had suggested Glenna as a travelling companion. Fud had told him she was bringing Vincent's Cortina.

'Good grief, she's about fourteen! I thought he was married, this Vincent?'

Danny confirmed that he was indeed married and that his wife was a Green Lady.

'Like in Tretchikoff, you mean?'

'No, like in District Nurse, stupid.' It was nice for Danny to feel superior for a change. He had gleaned the information from Fud. 'She drives around the outlying hamlets with a boot-load of pills and pamphlets showin' first-time mothers how to fold nappies and avoid it happenin' to them again.' Noreen's vocation was not without some irony in view of her inability, despite twenty-two years of marriage, to produce a son and heir or even – God forbid – a daughter for Vincent to brag about.

'What's he doing with a girlfriend then? Or am I just being boringly "Home Counties"?'

He kept his eyes level with the mattress and agreed that he, too, found the whole thing morally reprehensible. He'd now graduated from sleeping in the bath, but his elbows were getting skint off the carpet. When was she going to melt and let him into that bed with her?

Danny returned to the question of the Jubilee Tour, but here too his powers of persuasion seemed to have no effect on Suzi.

'They're not going to let this Glenna out of school to go on a rock'n'roll tour. Don't be stupid, McGlone.'

He could tell this was a diversionary tactic. 'Look, stop talkin' about her as if she was a schoolgirl – she's a grown woman, the lassie.' That didn't sound quite right, somehow. 'In fact, if you must know, she's an expectant mother.' It slipped out before he could stop himself.

Suzi's reaction was predictable. 'The rotten sod. And his wife's to be stuck at home with the kids – is that the idea?'

He told her they didn't have any kids. 'His wife's got somethin' up with her tubes.' He saw her head lift off the pillow. 'Or so Fud was saying.' He didn't want her to think that he'd been personally probing into Noreen's medical history.

'I don't imagine *she* knows about Glenna tagging along?'

Danny was beginning to wish he'd never brought the name up. 'You must be kiddin'. She'd kill him.' He tried to find a fluffier bit of the carpet for his elbows. 'If she ever finds out this doll's pregnant she'll probably kill the lot of us for keepin' it dark.' He'd decided to include Kettles in this potential bloodbath now that she was privy to the Munchkin being pregnant.

'So would I – you're a despicable bunch. And there's not an earthly that I'm coming on this stupid Jubilee Tour of yours!' She sounded like she meant it.

What'd she expect them to do, Danny thought, shop the guy? 'Don't lump me in with Vincent. I don't admire him any more than you do, Susan.' The use of her Sunday name was a calculated risk. He wanted into that bed beside her. 'A damn sight less, if you must know.' The catch in his voice was genuine – his elbows were now giving him gyp.

Suzi was suitably mollified. 'Yeah, I'm sorry, Danny.'

He felt her hand brush his hairdo. . . . He waited a few seconds. 'He still cannae get the chords for "Sweet Little Sixteen" right, and *he's* got the book.' Danny reached up to haul himself into bed, but Suzi had thrown back the covers and raced for the bathroom before he could get his leg over the edge of the mattress. It must've been that third cup of cocoa, he thought. He felt the warmth left by her body on the back of his thighs. Even if she decided against coming out on the road with them, he would at least have the memory of this night's bliss to see him through the next several weeks.

He lay back and waited.

And waited.

'Suzi?'

She spat savagely into the basin and squeezed another dollop of toothpaste onto the brush. She really could pick them, couldn't she?

'It wasnae like this when the flower of Britain's young manhood was waitin' to set off for Flanders.'

Danny McGlone's voice sounded a million miles away.

Suzi stuck the toothbrush back in the tumbler and wrenched open the medicine cabinet. She reached up and took down the carton she'd bought at the chemist's the day before. If she was going to find out, now was as good a time as any. The instructions on the side of the nondescript box were in English, German, Spanish and Portuguese. So it didn't only happen if you were Scottish? There was little comfort to be had from the joke. She broke the seal and took out the plastic beaker. She placed it on the toilet seat, and laid the packet containing the litmus strips on the soap dish. Then she closed her eyes and clung to the towel rail.

'Even so-called Nice Girls were happy to supply a little Rumpy-Pumpy!' the voice went on inexorably.

Suzi reached out a hand and groped for the packet of litmus papers.

★

'Where are we, Dennis?' In the back of the Transit Bomba's eyes were tight shut.

'Approachin' Kirkcaldy.' The sea mist slunk in from the shore and transformed the coal bings ahead into a Hokusai woodcut. A bandy-legged ten-year-old with a black face stuck out a pink slug of a tongue and manoeuvred a pramload of coal round the squashed remains of a rabbit lying in the roadway with its guts protruding from its middle like a wet, red hanky. He gave it a prod with his stove-in trainer as he passed. The flattened thing oozed some greyish fluid onto the road. The trainee miner gave a short laugh and stood on the rabbit's skull. There was a faint cracking sound. That cheered him up no end and he went on his way, shoving his pram and whistling the theme from *Watership Down*. Dennis pressed his boot to the floor and shot a glance in the rear-view mirror. The Munchkin was still tailing them, Danny observed. He couldn't help wishing it was Suzi Kettles back there in the clapped-out Cortina.

'Anybody needin' to go to the toilet just give us a bell.' Dennis liked to observe the niceties, though how they were supposed to deal with this little problem at seventy miles an hour was quite another matter. Dennis stopped for nobody.

They all said thanks, they were quite happy to sit in abject misery till they got to Methil, the first stop on what was advertised as 'The Majestics' Triumphant Silver Jubilee Tour'.

'Eddie took the wife and I for a bite to eat at this Greek joint last night. Talk about murder!' Dennis screwed his face into a passable imitation of a Japanese Noh actor with very painful piles. 'Murder' was a favourite Majestics' cover-all word, Danny had noticed.

'Give us a shout if you pass a phone box.' Bomba obviously talked in his sleep – his eyes were still shut.

You could hear the cut-out bits in Dennis's brain functioning, Danny thought with amused contempt.

'No, I had the hummus and chips. It was the wife that had the phone box.'

Vincent stifled a yawn. Fud placed a black nine on top of the jack of hearts.

'Hey, you're never goin' to believe what Eddie ordered at this Greek dive!' There were no takers first time round, so Dennis repeated himself.

This time Fud rose to the bait. 'What?' He took the black nine off the red jack and placed it on top of the eight of spades. The Majestics clearly had their own way of playing solitaire.

'Kebabs.' Dennis glanced in the mirror to note Fud's reaction.

Fud removed the nine of clubs and put it in his pocket.

Nothing daunted, the roadie persevered. 'Straight up, word of honour, kebabs.'

There was a lengthy silence broken only by Bomba's gentle snores.

Vincent ran an exploratory hand down the back of his DA, possibly to check if his head was on the right way round. 'So?'

'Kebabs, Vincent?' Dennis took his eyes off the road for a second and aimed a meaningful look at the Majestics' guitar ace.

Vincent's expression did not alter one iota.

'I don't think you heard me right, Vincent.' Dennis checked his rear-view mirror. 'He ordered kebabs. *Kebabs*, yeah?'

In the three weeks since the funeral, Danny mused, he hadn't heard one of these dummies utter a word of regret over Big Jazza's untimely demise, let alone the exact manner of his departure. The time had obviously come.

'Kebabs, Vinnie.'

Danny saw Bomba's eyelids flicker. Of course they missed the Big Guy. You don't play together for twenty-five years without there being some sort of deep bonding process. They just had their own way of articulating it.

'Did I hear somebody mention kebabs?' The drummer propped himself up on one elbow.

'That's what Eddie ordered last night. Kebabs. No kiddin', Bomba.'

Danny sneaked his hanky out of his pocket in readiness.

'Aw, I thought you had some in the wagon, the way you were talkin'. I havenae had a kebab in Christ-knows-how-long.' Bomba's head fell back again.

As Danny stuffed the hanky up his sleeve he wished fervently that he could stuff the Majestics' Silver Jubilee Tour up Eddie Clockerty's jaxie.

★

'I'll go and ask. . . .'

Vincent leaped out of his chair in the Residents' Lounge and grabbed Glenna by the arm. 'You do and I'll. . . .' He raised his fist.

Two bright spots appeared on Glenna's cheeks. 'You'll what?'

Vincent hesitated.

'You'll *what*, Diver?' Glenna was beginning to wish she'd never got involved with this middle-aged moron.

Vincent lowered his fist and shoved the tiny Glenna into a seat. His voice was like a serrated knife as he bent and placed his face close to hers. 'I warned you that life on the road was goin' to be tough. . . .' His jaw muscles started to grind. His eyes narrowed until they were tiny slits slashed across his cheekbones. Glenna drew back and waited for the explosion. When it came the very chair in which she sat trembled.

★

'That is stunning, Danny. Absolutely stunning.'

Danny would have preferred to see it with the trousers on rather than just his washed-in boxer shorts and his bare legs hanging down like Gargantua's links, but he had to agree it was pretty breathtaking. Yes, he thought, silver lamé looks good even when it's pinned together on a big frame and trying to kid on it's three sizes smaller than it is. For some reason he was reminded of Dürer's engraving of a rhinoceros.

'How're we doing on the trouser front, Miss Toner?' Eddie looped the tailor's tape around his neck and pinned the coat under the oxters.

'I'm not workin' on the front, I'm workin' on the seat – is that not what you told me?' Janice sat on the hotel bed with Big Jazza's last pair of bespoke peg-bottoms piled up in her lap like a great puddle of quicksilver.

'It feels kinda creepy,' Danny said, shivering slightly.

Eddie was uncharacteristically solicitous. 'Whereabouts, Danny son?' He trotted round to the back of the coat.

'No, I mean wearin' somethin' that was intended for a. . . .'

'Cadaver?' One could always trust Miss Toner. 'Yeah, that's just what I was thinkin'.' She bit off a length of thread and aimed it at the needle.

Eddie remonstrated with her. What were they supposed to do – cut it up for hankies?

'It wouldnae make into hankies, Mr Clockerty.' She pulled a face. 'It's like sandpaper.'

Eddie assured Danny it was going to look wonderful under the lights. 'Believe me, Danny son, if you and the boys don't upstage. . . .' He stopped himself.

'Upstage who, Eddie?' What was he talking about?

Eddie dropped a box of pins. 'Sorry, Danny?' he said absent-mindedly.

'He means upstage the top-of-the-bill, don't you, Mr C?' Janice made her seventh attempt at threading her needle.

'You . . .' He jabbed a finger at Janice, 'are getting the next train home, m'lady.' Then he was off, into the bathroom, and the door shut smartly behind him.

What was it about him, Danny wondered. Every time he opened his gub somebody ran into a bathroom and snibbed the door.

★

Fud O'Donnell wandered across the lounge, pausing only to sniff at the bowl of polypropylene hyacinths on the coffee table. They smelt strongly of haddock. He sat down between Vincent and Glenna. He didn't look at Glenna, but gave the guitarist a smile.

'Hi. We've ordered afternoon tea.' Vincent turned his face to the wall. Trust O'Donnell to bugger everything up.

Bomba poked his head into the lounge, did a double-take, then swaggered over to join them. He didn't look at Diver but gave Glenna a smile. 'When're you off back to Glasgow, sweetheart?'

Trying to retain a modicum of dignity, Glenna gathered up her belongings. 'I'm goin' upstairs. Excuse me.'

Bomba leaned back in his chair. 'Don't worry, Vinnie. I'll manage to eat for *three*.'

They watched Glenna teeter across the lounge in her stiletto-heeled bootees and leather mini, bump into the doorpost and disappear into the lobby.

'You . . .' The drummer placed a finger lightly on the shoulder of his brother-in-law's leather jacket, 'are a bastard, Diver.'

Vincent shrugged the finger off.

'Havin' a bit on the side is one thing – two houses, that I can turn a blind eye to – but when you go and do the *real* dirty on my young sister that cannae have any kids. . . .' Bomba got to his feet.

'Aw, get stuffed.' Vincent stood up and smoothed the skin-tight jeans down his spindly shanks.

The drummer's powerful arm shot out and grabbed a fistful of Diver's shirt.

'Dump her!' Bomba's nose was touching the guitar player's.

Their eyes locked.

'Will I hell!' Vincent's jaw muscles clenched. 'I asked her to come on this tour and she's comin' . . . *all* the way.' He brought his arm up suddenly and knocked Bomba's hand away.

A shower of shirt buttons hit the floor.

Vincent's head went down. It came up, blazing. 'Look what you've done – you've tore all my buttons off, ya moron!'

Bomba peeled his lips back, bared his teeth and shoved them into Vincent's face.

'It's somethin' else that'll get tore off the next time.'

The guitar player blenched. 'Away to hell.' He turned on his lizard-skin heel and headed for the door.

'Well, what d'you think?' Now dressed in the entire Bacofoil ensemble, Danny wanted to give the rest of the band a preview before the sound check.

But Vincent Diver strode past him on the hotel landing without so much as a second glance.

What did Danny care? *He* knew he was looking like a million bucks. *Diver?* He didn't even appear to have any buttons on his shirt.

Danny eased the trouser seat away from his bum, strolled nonchalantly downstairs and turned into the Residents' Lounge. He was feeling on top of the world again, and reminded himself to give Suzi Kettles a phone at some juncture.

'Well, what d'you think?'

O'Donnell and MacAteer had just taken delivery of a big tray of goodies and a teapot, and Danny's appearance in the silver suit had the desired effect. Fud choked on his French cake and Bomba's tea went down the wrong way. Danny sat down and selected what he considered to be a cheeky-looking meringue.

'What's this about the Majestics not headlinin'?' He bit into his prize – in retrospect not a good idea, because when Bomba told him who it was that they were playing second fiddle to the cream came straight down his nose and went all over his good shiny pegs.

The Tartan Lads?! Sufferin' God....

★

'I'm just after tellin' you.' Glenna planted another batch of kisses on Vincent's stringy throat.

'Tellin' me what?' Vincent brought his left arm out from under the blanket and sneaked a glance at his watch.

'That I want to stay with the tour. That's what you want, isn't it?' Glenna augmented the kisses with a nibble at his Adam's apple.

'Er ... yeah, sure, baby ... sure I do.' Vincent reached under the covers and tried to hitch his jeans over his knees.

'I love you, Vincent.' Glenna wrapped her arms around the guitarist's naked shoulders and gave his earlobe a bite.

Vincent recognised the signal and threw back the bedclothes. 'Sorry, babe, but you know what Clockerty's like if I'm not there to oversee these sound checks.' He tugged desperately at his 501s.

Glenna watched him throw on his shirt and buckle his belt rather too tightly.

'So that's it, settled. You're goin', right?' he said.

Glenna jack-knifed into a sitting position. 'I'm *what*?'

Vincent tried to button his buttonless shirt. His sleekit eyes looked innocently down at the makeshift bed on the carpet. 'Is that not what we agreed, doll?' ...

In the next-door bedroom Janice adjusted the volume on her Sony Walkman and tried to concentrate on the Bananarama file in the *Smash Hits*. Eddie stirred slightly in the adjacent twin bed. The muffled screaming from the adjoining bedroom grew louder. Something hard and heavy banged against the thin partition wall, and there was a sound of breaking glass.

Janice tossed the *Smash Hits* onto the bedside table and removed the headphones from her ears. Raising her voice, she yelled: 'If you don't jack that in I'm getting the management.'

Eddie turned over and crammed his head under the pillow. The ear-piercing screams reached a climax, then there was a dull thump followed by silence.

Janice waited a few seconds, then reached over and gave Eddie's back a dunt with her foot. 'Here....' She held out the headphones. 'D'you want to listen to *The Magic Flute*, Mr Clockerty?'

★

Fud plucked at the silent bass strings as he waited for Dennis to get some juice going so he could get his fingers limbered up. 'Maybe Vincent and the girlfriend's beat it, no?'

'No, the Cortina's still in the hotel car park.' Dennis did his best to unfankle the amp leads.

How the hell had they managed to get in this mess, Danny wondered.

'How come there was no answer when I chapped his bedroom door, then?' Fud's knuckles were all red.

'Perhaps he was ... busy?' The Majestics' roadie gave 'busy' the lewdest possible coloration and he got a toe in the backside from Bomba. '*Ohyah!*'

Danny ran his fingers up and down the mute keys just for the exercise. He couldn't blame Vincent for playing hookey – some Silver Jubilee Tour this was shaping up to be. According to Eddie, they'd been supposed to be going out as headliners. 'I reckon we'll all have to sit down and have a serious talk with His Holiness,' he ventured.

There was a good deal of hilarity at this. Even Fud laughed.

'Forget it, Danny Boy.' Bomba beat out a tattoo on his hi-hat. 'The one and only time we sat down with Eddie, we finished up handin' him back our wages.'

'Aye, it's never Eddie's fault. He'll be puttin' the blame on to Wee Tommy Cairns and Carntyne Promotions for this fiasco the night.' Fud cocked an ear, then adjusted his silent bottom string.

Bomba switched from the hi-hat to the side drum. 'He's still puttin' the blame on to Wee Tommy for our one and only hit single.'

Danny remembered the single well. Number seven in the *NME* charts, 1962. Stayed there for nine weeks. He had a flashback of his Maw running down to the Co-operative with the page torn out of the paper to show to the butcher. The teacher used to ask him to stand up in class and sing it. But he wasn't sure what Bomba was saying now. 'Blamed him for the fact it was your one and only?' Danny pressed.

It was Fud who burst the bubble. 'Eddie maintains that if only Wee Tommy hadnae bought all *his* copies from the one shop it would've went higher up the hit parade than it did.'

Was Danny hearing right above the racket? 'You're not goin' to tell me....'

Bomba picked up the story with what he thought was unseemly relish. 'There just wasnae enough mugs – sorry, record buyers – goin' out of their way to snap up the Majestics' very first waxing, so what Wee Tommy and Eddie done....'

Danny didn't think he wanted to hear all this.

O'Donnell butted in. 'Set Wee Tommy back four and a half grand.'

Danny was shattered. He'd always believed that was the one thing nobody could take away from Big Jazza and the Majestics, a number seven hit single. And now it turned out it was hyped into the charts.

'I'm still not gettin' nothin' here, Dennis.' Fud plucked at the Rickenbacker without getting any joy.

'Stop gangin' up on us. It's that bloody piano, it's sappin' all the voltage.' Dennis fiddled with the keyboard circuits. 'Where the hell *is* Vincent? He's got the manual for this contraption.'

Fud volunteered to nip back to the hotel and winkle Diver out. Danny hunted disconsolately through his pockets for some 10ps to phone Suzi. What was the betting there wasn't a Santa Claus either?

★

Vincent took the phone from the receptionist. 'You sure it's for me?'

The receptionist's lips parted in a grimace. 'If you wouldn't be too long, that's the taxi phone.'

Vincent turned his collar up and ran a hand over his blue-black hairdo. 'Hullo?'

It was a woman's voice but faint.

'Give who a message?' Vincent asked. 'Aw, him.... Aye, if I see him.' He sniffed. 'What'd you say your name was again?' Vincent sniggered. 'Sure, yeah, I'll tell him you rang....' He went to put down the phone, then hesitated. 'Hey, listen, Suzi....' He let his voice slip down a few notches into the Bob Mitchum drawl he'd perfected into his cassette recorder. 'Has anybody ever told you what a sexy number you sound over the telephone?'

There was a click followed by a purring noise.

Vincent held the receiver away from his ear, then slammed it back on its cradle. 'Dolls, who needs them?' He fingered the dried blood on his cheek, a souvenir from Glenna before he'd finally persuaded her to up stumps and go. Still, Bomba had threatened a good deal worse. Vincent had just started for the door when the phone rang and he hopped smartly back....

'Hullo, sexy tonsils, what say you and me get together and....' He stopped.

The gruff voice at the other end of the line sounded distinctly unfriendly.

Vincent dropped the Mitchum drawl and the telephone. 'There's some balloon wantin' a taxi here,' he muttered to no one in particular, and then beat a hasty retreat before the receptionist reappeared.

★

What is it with jugglers, he wondered. Twenty minutes Danny'd been queuing at that payphone, and this guy they were sharing the gig with was still engaged in a rambling conversation with his agent. All he wanted to say to Suzi was 'I love you, Kettles' – it wouldn't have taken a minute.

'What're you botherin' for?' Fud rubbed the pomade well into his hands, then applied them to his bonzo. 'She never thought to phone *you*, did she?'

That was true.

'Take my advice, get yourself a hobby.' He massaged his scalp so hard that his face bounced up and down.

Danny asked what'd happened to the others – they had to be due on shortly, no? He tried to sound cool, but he could see his lips trembling in the manky mirror ... just.

'Bomba's away gettin' his shirt pressed and Vinnie's along bein' sick.'

Thank God for that. He thought he was the only one that was nervous, he joked. He clamped a hand to his jaw to stop his teeth chattering.

O'Donnell ran a gumsy comb through his well-greased locks. 'No, Vinnie isnae nervous. He's just bein' sick, Danny Boy.'

Danny looked around the dressing room. He was not surprised. Another earwig wove its way across the crappy counter top, but he didn't have the heart to squash it. He didn't have the stomach for it, either. There was already a pile of corpses about an inch high next to his empty fag packet. What d'you do with a pile of earwig corpses, he wondered. He thought about spreading them on toast and giving the delicacy to Vincent. No, that would be cannibalism, wouldn't it?

He tapped a cigarette off Fud. Who was it they were on after, again?

'The vent.' Fud had to grab hold of Danny's wrist while he lit his cigarette off the shaky match. 'The one with the "lifelike dummy, Fiona".'

Danny wondered if this could be the same Fiona that he'd just been chatting up out at the payphone. She wasn't in the least 'lifelike', he thought – who was the vent trying to kid? ... It seemed to take him ages to light up from the shoogly match.

Bomba breenged through the dressing room door, nearly giving Danny a heart attack. He was carrying a freshly ironed shirt on a wire coathanger. 'Don't tell us you're nervous, Danny Boy?'

What, him, *nervous*?

Bomba took the Benson's out of Danny's gub, turned it round and handed it back. So *that* was what the funny taste was. Danny gave the drummer a wan smile.

Then the roadie stuck his ugly mug round the door. 'You're on!'

Buggeration.

'Shame you don't have time to make that call, innit?'

Danny felt like punching him.

★

'I told you that suit would look fabulous under the lights.'

Considering it had been his official Silver Jubilee Tour debut and they'd got on and off without getting pelted with coal briquettes, Danny thought their manager could have elaborated just a little.

They stood there in the Miners' Welfare car park with only two feet between them, but the gulf was unbridgeable. The blue wisp of cigarette smoke curlicued into the deeper blue of the night sky. Danny cocked an ear – the Tartan Lads were well into their wind-up medley now.

His eye followed the spiralling fag smoke and he thought of the uncommunicative Suzi Kettles. 'What is it with dolls, eh?'

Eddie was thoughtful for a long time. 'Now you're asking, Danny son.'

At least he hadn't called him 'Danny *Boy*' – that and 'The Dark Island' played at a funereal pace on an amplified accordion could well have put the tin lid on how he was feeling. As it was, the smoke from the cigarette was already making his eyes water. Always have a fag handy when you get the blues – it's the perfect cover-up.

Gin a Body Dig a Body

The small bunch of shrivelled pansies lay, not where the prop man had placed it, but about eighteen inches camera left of the bashed-in end of the bus shelter, where the director had a hunch it would make 'a more telling frame' when the documentary featurette on the Majestics was spliced together. He had, however, neglected to tell Sheena Fisher what he'd done.

'"No Particular Place to Go"....' The ex-model, ex-local radio ombudsperson strolled hands in pockets in the direction of the bus shelter as the four-man film crew backed slowly along the gutter ahead of her. 'A rare archive clip of the Glasgow-based band performing the Chuck Berry number back in 1964.' Fingers crossed the BBC could lay hands on the promised footage. Sheena Fisher timed the smile of sympathy to perfection. 'And it was here in this quiet residential street ...' she raised her voice above the traffic noise, 'just six weeks ago that Jazza McGlone, the Majestics' extrovert singer, discovered that "No Particular Place" meant precisely that when the Ford Sierra he was driving crashed headlong into this bus shelter....' Her gaze dropped to the wet pavement, 'at over seventy miles an hour. Dammit. Sorry, Duggie, can we go back on that? Some idiot's moved the bloody flowers.'

'Cut.'

★

'Let me out and I'll thumb a lift home, okay?'

You don't see hide nor hair of a doll for a fortnight, Danny fumed, and that's the slant the conversation takes? He was wondering if it had been such a good idea to pick Ms Kettles up and take her on location in Glasgow after all. He didn't fancy turning up at the death locus any more than she did, but this was going to be his movie debut.

Dennis broke in: 'Eddie says there's every likelihood it'll get networked, this tribute.'

What did he mean 'tribute'? Eddie hadn't mentioned anything to Danny about a tribute when he'd telephoned their bottom-of-the-lucky-bag digs in We-Never-Sleep Ardrossan at midnight and told him to get himself back to Glasgow at the crack of dawn.

'The only bus shelter hereabouts is in Berryhill Drive – s'that any use to you?' The milkman Dennis had stopped

to ask the way from had a face like an unrisen cottage loaf.

Danny had to hang on to Kettles to stop her climbing out of the Transit.

'Thanks, pal.' Dennis wound up the window and started barking at Danny about getting himself into a state.

It wasn't him that was getting into a state, he protested, it was Kettles.

Dennis swung the Transit the wrong way round a roundabout and up a cul-de-sac. They reversed out over a toddler's trike.

His suspicions aroused, Danny hoped it wasn't all going to be about the Big Guy. He was certainly going to look a right poultice in the tartan suit he'd borrowed off the widowed Theresa if it was.

★

The buzz and clatter of sewing machines from the floor below Wee Tommy's office was deafening. Eddie screwed up a corner of a one-armed T-shirt and inserted the point in his ear.

'Have you got the message bag with the rest of them in it, Miss Toner?' Eddie thought it might be wise to double-check each faulty item before bearding the Carntyne Promotions boss in his den.

Janice snapped her compact shut, slung it back in her handbag and took out a traffic-stopping red lipstick.

'Well, if you havenae got it it'll still be under the stairs on the bus, willn't it?' The lipstick popped obscenely out of its tube.

The Majestics' manager threw up his hands in exasperation. 'Good grief, lassie....'

A girl in a nylon overall pushed open the door. 'What one of you's Mr Clockerty?'

Janice pouted her traffic-stopping lips. The girl turned to Eddie.

Eddie brandished the one-armed T-shirt. 'Are you responsible for this?'

The girl gave the offending garment the once-over. 'I'm kiddies' nightwear.' She turned the T-shirt over and read the legend '25 and Still Royally Rockin'' without much interest. 'Mr Cairns says you've to see yourselves off the premises.' She turned her head slightly as they heard a large car pull almost soundlessly away from the front of the building.

Eddie galloped across to the window.

The girl held the black T-shirt by its solitary sleeve and regarded the crudely drawn likenesses of Danny, Bomba, Fud and Vincent with mild curiosity. 'What are these for, anyhow – a funeral party?'

★

What else could Danny say? They hadn't called his brother 'The Beast of Rock' for nothing. As far as he knew, the invalid already had his napper down the toilet while Big Jazza was still onstage at that particular gig, and as for the stories about him poking the eyes out of goldfish and biting the thumbs off slumbering infants, well, those were mostly conjecture, weren't they?

'And cut.'

What did this Fisher chick want him to tell her, that Big Jazza was a daily communicant and a collector for the St Vincent de Paul Society?

'A little more volume next time, Donny.'

The McGlone hackles rose. If there was one thing he hated, it was people getting his name wrong. Especially, he thought, TV directors called Duggie. Danny told him the doll was just after telling him to keep it *down*. 'And it's Danny, not Donny, *Doogie*.' He didn't see why the tube should get off with it – he didn't have to put up with that garbage.

'How're we doin', Kettles? Fascinatin', innit?'

'What're you playing at?' she hissed. 'He was your brother, for God's sake. *She's* getting paid to do a hatchet job – you aren't.'

Before the innocent Danny could reach forward and wring Suzi's neck, Sheena Fisher came up and dragged him away.

'I think we'll do the next piece inside the shelter, Danny.' He could see how this doll got picked up for TV – he just hoped she had the savvy to realise he wasn't trying to upstage the scene of the accident with the tartan suit.

'It's only rock'n'roll, Suzi,' Danny tossed over his shoulder, but he couldn't see where she'd gone. He presumed she'd dollied round the bus shelter to get a better angle.

Next time, he thought, he wanted one of those deckchairs with his name on it.

★

The Majestics' bass player took a deep breath before entering the Gents' Sitting Room, where he found the lead guitarist studying the thinning patch in his Tony Curtis coiffure in the convex mirror above the flesh-tiled mantelpiece. Fud tried to sound casual.

'Eddie wasnae there. I had a word with Janice.'

Vincent cracked his finger joints in acknowledgement and crossed to the window.

'Know what they went back to Glasgow for?' Fud fell into an armchair and swung his leg over the side. 'To make a TV movie.' He watched the guitar player wipe the windowpane with the curtain. 'All about Danny Boy.'

Vincent scanned the seaside street for any sign of the Cortina. A child in a pixie hood solemnly bounced a large beachball off the kerb and licked the melting ice cream

running down the sides of the pokey hat it held in its free hand. It was a depressing picture.

'So Janice was sayin'. I've just spoke to her on the phone,' Fud reiterated. He plucked nervously at the uncut moquette. 'And they've got all these T-shirts with Danny Boy's kisser all over them – away and phone her yourself if you don't believe me.'

Vincent let his lips unpucker in disbelief. 'She's pullin' your leg, O'Donnell.'

Fud picked up the landlady's cardigan and buffed his loafers. 'She didnae sound like she was pullin' anybody's leg, Vinnie.'

'I'll talk to her,' Vincent said in a shaky voice. He tried not to run to the door.

'Don't say who it was that told you.' Fud stuffed the now soiled cardigan under the cushion.

Ding dong. Fud got up and crossed to the window.

Outside on the front step Glenna pressed the door chimes once more. She hadn't seen Vincent since the Methil gig, and felt sick with excitement. She pressed again ... and kept pressing. Some welcome this was.

⭐

Eddie had started to pace on the telephone's fourth ring.

'It's Vincent – I know it's Vincent. Any sensible person would've rung off by now.'

Janice reached for the phone. 'I'll tell him it was a mistake about the T-shirts, all right?'

Eddie's sweaty hand landed on top of hers. 'And how d'you explain about Danny and the TV, Miss Smarty-pants?'

'Don't be daft – they're all goin' to see that when it comes out.' Janice was losing patience with Clockerty's histrionic behaviour. 'Besides, I heard you tellin' that wee creep Cairns that they were all goin' to be featured in it – the whole band – so what's the beef?'

Eddie's eyes rolled up under his lids. He thought he'd explained to the stupid girl that, while Danny was appearing in glorious technicolor, shot by a professional TV crew, the Majestics would merely be seen in scratchy black

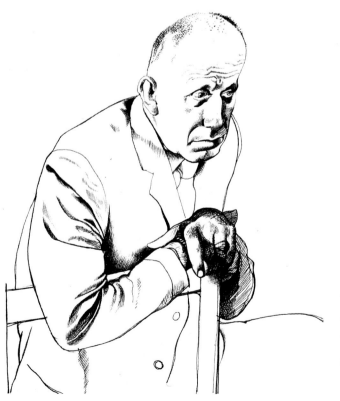

and white caught in some God-forsaken drill hall by Mrs Clockerty on a ten-bob home movie camera – *that* was the beef!

'"Archive footage" – you heard me saying it to Wee Tommy. "Archive footage", right?'

The phone continued to ring. Janice's patience evaporated. 'I'm a drapery assistant, not the Cambridge Street Film Buff of the Year! As far as I'm concerned, "archive footage" could just as well be them secondhand blue suede bumpers you're sellin' down the stair.'

'Listen.' Eddie's knuckles went white. The phone had stopped. 'Is that a good sign or a bad sign, d'you think?'

'You don't pay me nearly enough to think – work it out for yourself.' Janice withdrew her hand from the receiver, scowled and flounced to the door.

Eddie's face went the same colour as his matching tie and hanky. 'As soon as I've got your redundancy money together you're fired, m'lady!'

'Aw, shuttup.'

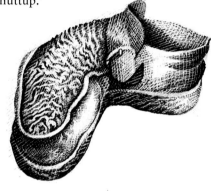

⭐

'You're a chum, Kettles.' Danny stretched out for the coffee. But why was she giving him two mugs?

'And you, McGlone, are an idiot.'

Why – because he'd gone for a few cocktails with his fellow technicians after the wrap? Kettles had skedaddled, hadn't she?

'What kind of state was *she* in when you left her?'

She? Who she?

'The Hatchet Woman.' Suzi's voice had a certain edge to it. 'I was at school with this cretin, bear in mind. She's got an O-level in perfidy.'

The coffee was very hot and Danny wondered why he was pouring it into his ear.

'God, if your mother could only see you now.'

He put a foot on the floor to stop the sofa from careering round the room. Holding on to it, he braced himself for the touchdown.

'Get your togs off, you're going under the shower.'

Why was this strange red-haired woman peeling off his coat and unhooking his galluses, he pondered in a curiously pleasant, semi-detached way. The floor came up and smacked him in the kisser.

'Don't forget to take your socks off.'

Over his shoes? Good trick.

Kettles must've rearranged the furniture since he was last in the apartment, Danny thought, because he kept bumping into it. Plus she'd had some undulating linoleum put down in the hall. Before he knew where he was he didn't know where he was. So he stood there in his shirt tail till the joint came to a halt. Ah, yes, his old bedroom. He recognised the enamel mattress.

'Get a move on. And there's no hot water, I'm afraid ... the immerser's on the blink.'

⭐

Janice made out another £1.99 price ticket and pinned it to the leg of the Johnny Sheffield surfing shorts. She'd already explained to Diver that Eddie wasn't available. 'D'you want me to put it in writin' for you?' She chucked the surfing shorts onto the 'Fire Sale' pile and picked up a sloppy joe with egg stains down the front.

Vincent snatched it out of her hand and slammed his fist down on the counter. 'I've drove all the way from Ardrossan and I've got a pregnant vocalist sittin' out there in that motor – tell Clockerty I want to see him about this TV movie he hasnae seen fit to tell us about!'

Janice leaned forward and peered through the dusty window of the shop.

Vincent swerved round the counter and made for the stairs. 'Where is he?' he bellowed. 'Up here?' The shoogly stairs protested under the onslaught from his furiously pounding reptilian footwear.

Janice strolled across to the window and moved the Billy Eckstein shirt boxes to one side. 'Aw, it's *her*. I never knew she was a vocalist.' She tried to remember Glenna's name, but couldn't. . . .

'I'll kill that stupid girl.' Upstairs Eddie cowered under his desk and muttered to himself.

The door frame shook and the glass panel in the door rattled. 'I know you're in there, ya midden!'

Eddie cringed.

'Are you goin' to open this door and have a civilised conversation or. . . .' Vincent stopped and placed his ear against the glass.

There was a faint whimper from inside.

'All right – if that's the way you want it.' Vincent backed off along the short length of passageway for his run-up.

Eddie poked his head out of his hideyhole. It was very quiet. Too quiet, surely?

Then there was an ear-splitting crash, a splintering of wood and an agonised '*Aaaaaaaaaaaaaaaaaaaaargh!*'

'Oh, my God!' Eddie crawled out from under the desk on all fours.

Vincent Diver was now standing inside the Clockerty Enterprises office, his hands clasped to his head. Blood oozed between his fingers.

Eddie clambered to his feet. His expression was one of mild surprise, his tone devoid of irony. 'Vincent.' He crunched his way across the broken glass, his hand extended. 'Was that you knocking?'

★

'Forget about Eddie.' Bomba eased his swollen feet out of his sodden crepes. It had been nice seeing Christine and the kids again, but it had been even nicer seeing them onto the train for home. He didn't want to think about Dennis and Danny Boy, Vincent or the Munchkin – he just wanted to plunge his aching feet into a basin of warm water before the gig at Ardrossan's Club Paradiso. 'Whatever needs sortin' out, I'll sort it out.'

Fud breathed a sigh of relief. 'Good, because the guy says unless the Majestics're onstage and ready to rock at twenty-five past seven you've to get kneecapped.'

Bomba's nose twitched. 'I've to get what?'

Fud started to explain about the electric drill technique but the drummer cut him short.

What did Fud mean, *he'd* to get kneecapped?

'I thought if I phoned the guy down the Club with the missin' ear and explained the situation' – Fud was almost apologetic – 'gave him your name and address, er. . . .'

'What situation?'

'How one or two of us might not make the gig, that was all – *aaaaaargh!*' The bass player found it difficult getting anything further out, with Bomba's hands round his windpipe.

Bomba's voice betrayed his panic. 'Supposin' Danny Boy doesnae get back in time?'

'Then we go with Vinnie and that chick Glenna. . . . Goin' to quit chokin' us?'

Bomba's pupils dilated in horror. 'You mean, you'd actually have a chick singer frontin' the Majestics?'

O'Donnell fell back into the armchair and rubbed his aching throat. If it was a choice between being able to walk out of the Paradiso and not being able to walk out, he didn't give a toss if it was a *chick pea* fronting the Majestics as long as it could open its gub and make a noise.

★

The Cortina mounted the nearside verge and bounced back onto the road. Glenna fought for control. 'What're all these people doin' in this car, anyhow?'

Vincent held on to his bandaged head. 'Because we want to get back to Ardrossan before it shuts, Glenna!' His face contorted in agony as the Cortina hit a pothole.

Eddie's voice in his left ear was concerned . . . 'Stitches still nipping a wee bit, old son?'

The Cortina wobbled alarmingly.

'Goin' to not talk to him while I'm drivin'?'

Janice clung to the back of the front seat, her normally chalk-white complexion tinged with citrus yellow. 'Did you say you wanted cremated when you went, Mr Clockerty? I cannae quite remember.'

The Cortina carved a slice out of the offside verge and narrowly missed a startled-looking sheep.

At the same time as the Cortina was hurtling onwards, a pale blue Transit was travelling in the same direction at approximately the same speed but on another road some fifty yards to the left. The two roads were not quite parallel, and they converged at an unmarked junction.

★

What was she telling Danny all this stuff now for, he wondered. That was what he'd taken her on location for, so she could stop him making a hash of it – which he hadn't, but which she was clearly implying he had.

'I did say something, ya lunkhead, only you were too besotted with Barbie Doll Fisher for it to sink in.' Dumb Danny, she thought, remembering the boys at school – a lot of putting out and nothing at the check-in with that chick.

Ha! I do believe she's jealous, Danny thought. . . . *Ooooooooooooow!* He reminded Dennis it was only a Transit he was steering towards Ardrossan, not the John Cobb Special attempting a wheelie.

'And to think I've just given up a bright future in cocktail waitressing to come on this trip.' Kettles tried her best to look despondent. 'Get a grip of yourself, McGlone.'

He realised he had the Mammy and Daddy of all hang-overs, but he didn't remember asking her to come.

'*Whoooooah!* What was that?' Suzi birled round and peered back along the road.

What was what? Danny sat up.

'We nearly ran into a car there.'

'Car?' The roadie articulated the word as though he had no notion what it signified.

'Did you not see it?' Kettles was starting to annoy Danny again. 'A purple car with people in it, going very fast – I'm almost positive.'

There certainly wasn't any car there now, Danny thought as he stared back down the road, purple or any other colour. It was all quite deserted. He began to wonder who it was that'd been drinking, him or the ex-cocktail waitress.

★

The film editor tapped the white Chinagraph pencil against his teeth, his eyes glued to the screen as the grainy Majestics footage gave way to Danny McGlone's colour-ful features.

Danny's voice was fractionally out of sync with his lip movements, but Sheena Fisher caught the film editor's wrist. 'Leave it.' She flipped over the pages of her notebook.

'I was only a kid at the time, so you can imagine the shock it was to discover that Eddie Clockerty and this other geek had actually hyped the single into the charts.'

Danny McGlone's voice was tinny, but to Sheena Fisher, sitting there making occasional notes, what it was saying was pure gold.

'Okay, so there's been a lot of that kinda chicanery before and since, but the Majestics?'

The film editor glanced at Sheena Fisher. This guy was a born actor, they were both thinking.

'It was like finding out that Hans Christian Andersen was a werewolf, or the Pope was a drag queen.' Sheena made another note. 'Plus there was all that dirty business involving payola, sexual favours and famous names – I must say I felt decidedly queasy when I dredged up that little piece of info. . . . I wonder where Kettles's away to?' Danny's eyes swivelled and he was looking straight into camera. His head jerked back as if he'd been punched. 'God, I got the fright of my life there, I thought for a second that camera was still. . . .' The screen went suddenly blank.

'I can run it again if you like.' The editor stuck the marker pencil behind his ear.

'There's some more footage I want Duggie to shoot.'

'That manager of theirs once sold me a shirt. Twenty-nine and eleven – wash like a hanky, he said.' The editor set the lever to 'Rewind'. 'I hope you nail the bastard.'

Sheena Fisher

★

Suzi followed Danny downstairs, where there was a great deal of strange activity. Bomba was running about like a scalded moggy, while Fud kept reaching down and check-ing his kneecaps.

'What was it before it was a boarding house?' Suzi asked as she stepped into the Gents' Sitting Room.

Danny quizzed Fud as to where Vincent was hiding since it was time they were down the Paradiso, but all Fud did was shout for Bomba to get a move on. They heard the loo flush, and then Bomba came crashing down the stairs yelling for everybody to get in the wagon and how come the engine wasn't running? He took one look at Suzi and asked Danny what *she* was doing there, for which he got what Danny felt was a well-earned dunt. There was still no sign of Diver.

'You neednae think she's gettin' access to the dressin' rooms, whoever she is.'

That first dunt obviously hadn't registered, thought Danny, so he gave him another, harder one.

'*Ohyah.*'

'I thought you said Vincent was the charmer?' Suzi flashed Danny a smile, and his heart flipped over.

Yeah, where *was* Vincent?

The next thing they knew they were all in the wagon and apparently breaking the land speed record to get to the dump known as the Paradiso. Vincent was obviously down there already, Danny surmised. He gave Suzi a hug, feeling pleased now that he'd thought to bring her along.

★

Janice bent forward in the dank scrub and tried to repair her make-up. It was now so dark she could hardly see her face in the crashed Cortina's wing mirror.

'We should all've got rushed to the infirmary in that jeep . . . look at my good stockin's.' She stuck out a leg.

Eddie sighed. 'That "jeep" happened to be a Land Rover.' He ignored Janice's loud sniff. He'd considered it extraordinarily courteous of the gentleman to have volunteered to phone the rescue services once he'd delivered Vincent and Whatever-her-name-was to the nearest hospital. Eddie was now wondering where that might be.... Kilmarnock, perhaps? Stranraer? Carlisle? He still wasn't quite sure what had happened. Not that Whatever-her-name-was required another vehicle within a radius of a hundred miles to show what a lousy driver she was, but Miss Toner seemed pretty adamant about the presence of another car, van or truck ... something in blue, she'd said ... in the vicinity of the junction at around the same time as – Janice interrupted his thoughts.

'What's that funny smell?' She gave another loud sniff.

Eddie smiled. 'You're in the country, Miss Toner.'

'Not *that* funny smell, that *other* funny smell ... d'you smell it?'

Eddie sniffed. He couldn't smell anything.

Janice shot him a sidelong glance. 'Have you been rubbin' that stuff into your scalp again, Mr Clockerty?'

There was a sudden, dull *whump*.

'*Waaaaaaaaaaaaaaaaaaah!*' Janice leaped away from the side of the Cortina as a cloud of yellow smoke billowed out from under the chassis.

Eddie scrambled down the bank and tumbled headlong into the ditch. 'Oh, my God!'

'I told you I smelt somethin'!' Janice looked on in fascinated horror as flames started to lick up the bodywork of Vincent's car.

★

The lighting state in the low-ceilinged room went from green to red, turning the Club Paradiso into Hades and the proprietor, an outsize man with one ear missing, into Beelzebub himself. He stood under a swaying fibreglass palm and stared unblinkingly at the cramped stage where Suzi and Danny were swapping lines on the opening verse of 'That'll Be the Day'. The one-eared man had paid for *four* Majestics, and that was precisely what he was getting.

As Danny went into the instrumental break Suzi sidled over and tried shouting above the racket. 'I think I'd prefer the Black'n'Decker ... these trousers are killing me!'

Danny could see what she meant. They were tight enough on Vincent, but on her they were ohyah!

His hands itched to abandon the keys, but he was conscious of the big guy under the palm tree watching them. He felt his shirt clinging to his back. What they would've done without Suzi he hesitated to think. He sent a silent prayer winging heavenwards for art school bands. If he'd loved this doll before, he was nuts about her now. Absolutely nuts.

Suzi Kettles raised a blue suede shoe and gave Danny a dunt just behind the knee. Their heads came together at the mike and their lips formed the first of the 'ooh, oohs' in the middle eight of the Majestics' opening number. The lighting state went to heliotrope and the big man under the ersatz palm reluctantly unplugged the extension cable on the electric drill.

★

It was an incongruous sight, Vincent sitting there by the bedside, his head bandaged, his face haggard, while Glenna lay propped up on her pillows looking quite robust.

She winced a little as Vincent's hand clutched hers. 'I'm fine. They're only keeping me in overnight for observation.' Her eyes never left his face. 'You better go, Vincent.'

'God, I didnae half get the wind up – you were the colour of them sheets.' Vincent glanced down to check that they still used white sheets on hospital beds. 'You sure you're okay?'

'I love you, Vincent.'

Vincent Diver leaned over the bed and kissed her. 'I love me too.'

Glenna giggled. 'Go. You'll be late.'

Vincent became serious. 'You look after yourself. I want you up there beside me at the next gig, okay?' As he backed away from the bed he couldn't get over how young she looked.

'I'll bring the motor first thing in the mornin', all right?' He blew her a kiss.

Glenna caught it and blew it back. Her lips formed the words 'I love you.' Then she waved.

Vincent slipped between the screens and was gone.

★

When the new Majestics got back to the boarding house after the gig they were all in deliriously high spirits, especially Suzi who wisely chose to repair to the upstairs toilet to calm down. While Danny was drawing her a route map on the lobby wallpaper, Bomba, Fud and Dennis withdrew into the Gents' Sitting Room to finish off their chips. Due to Danny's feeble grasp of the layout of the house it was a full minute before Suzi could be dispatched aloft and he could join the other guys. When he pushed open the sitting room door and clocked Diver sitting there in the crepe-bandage bunnet he burst out laughing. What was it, some practical joke? Then it dawned on him that Bomba, Fud and Dennis were standing there with their faces tripping them. What was going on?

'I've just come from the hospital.' Vincent stood up and faced Danny. His voice was rough-edged.

Danny's eyes dove to the carpet. He felt terrible. 'I'm really sorry, Vincent,' he managed to mumble. 'What was it, a frontal lobotomy?'

There wasn't a titter.

'See if anythin' happens to this kid, I'm holdin' you directly responsible!' The injured guitar player took a step towards Danny.

Danny's brow furrowed. He glanced over his shoulder, but there was nobody at his back. What kid? It was a second before the penny dropped. Now Danny understood. The poor guy was obviously concussed. He was talking about himself ... regressive behaviour brought about by whoever or whatever had skelped him on the napper. Only Danny couldn't quite grasp what it had to do with *him*.

Vincent took another breenge in Danny's direction, but this time Fud and Bomba stepped forward and restrained him.

'Take it easy, Vinnie,' said Fud, while apparently trying to dislocate Diver's shoulder.

Bomba had a good grip of Vincent's other arm.

'I'll murder him ... let us go and I'll murder him!' screamed the hapless Vincent, trying to free himself. Fud and Bomba hung on grimly.

'Danny?' They could hear Suzi coming downstairs.

Danny pinched a handful of Dennis's chips and stuffed them into his mouth. 'In here, Kettles,' he shouted. 'Come and tell us if you don't think this looks like Daffy Duck.'

Vincent let out a loud squawk. Which was nothing compared to his reaction when Suzi strolled into the room. It took Fud and Bomba all their time to hold on to him. He seemed to go completely bananas. He ranted and raved and foamed at the mouth. It was a puzzlement to Danny ... she looked far better in that stage suit of Diver's than he'd ever done.

★

Back in Glasgow, at Manhattan Casuals, Sheena Fisher took a deep breath and opened her notebook. 'And you are?'

Janice chucked the last remaining pair of Sal Mineo cover-alls onto a shelf and leaned against the counter. 'I'm his amanuensis.'

Eddie bounced down the stairs, pulling on his jacket with the cuffs and the hand-stitched lapels. He stretched out a hand and introduced himself as he hit the bottom tread. He gave Sheena a big smile. 'You must be ...?'

'Fed up waitin',' Janice butted in. 'I'll go and kid on I'm tidyin' up, will I?' She moved away from the counter.

Eddie and Sheena Fisher watched her go.

'I asked them for a boy, and that's what they sent me.' Eddie shook his head while Sheena attempted a sympathetic rustle of her notepad. Eddie turned to face his unexpected visitor.

The camera man parked across the street zoomed in on the plate-glass window for a two-shot.

★

Glenna lay quite still in the bed, a porcelain doll.

Vincent's forearm ploughed a space among the balls of baby wool on top of the bedside cabinet. He laid the soggy poke of grapes and the 'special offer' Lucozade tablets in the centre of the Formica.

'It's okay. I know what you're goin' to tell me.' Glenna's was a small voice at the best of times.

Vincent scraped the chair across the waxed linoleum. He straddled it cowboy-style and vented his frustration by punching his fist into his palm. 'I told her not to bother to come, but she's got a week's holiday saved up.'

'Just promise me one thing, Vincent.'

'Sure, babe, anythin'.' He gave up the palm-punching and placed a horny hand on the doll's downy cheek.

'Promise me you willnae sleep with her.'

Vincent was dismayed. 'But she's my wife, Glenna.'

'Promise me.' Glenna's voice turned hard.

A crisp-aproned nurse swept through the screens, bringing with her a whiff of antiseptic, floor polish and overdone cabbage.

'Okay, okay, I promise.' Vincent's hand dropped from Glenna's cheek.

'Right then, Mr Diver.' The nurse pulled out her charge's covers, then tucked them back in. 'If we can just let Mrs Diver have her mid-morning nap now.' She lifted Glenna's head and punched the pillows up.

Glenna settled back. 'No, I'm not Mrs Diver.' She closed her eyes. The ghost of a smile hovered around her pale lips '... *Yet*.'

★

Don't You Rock Me, Daddy-o

'I cannae possibly eat these, they're stoatin'.' Janice sat up in her berth and banged one of the ginger snaps on the edge of the tray. The King's Cross to Aberdeen sleeper thundered into a tunnel.

Eddie Clockerty hung his face over the top bunk. 'Try dunkin' them.'

'Try whattin' them?'

'Dunkin' them!' After the abortive trip to London Eddie was on a very short fuse.

'Don't shout. It's not my fault you never got your stupid injunction to stop that dopey film. I don't know what we went all the way down to London for in the first place. I could've told you you wouldnae get it.'

'Shuttup, Janice.'

A shower of biscuit crumbs pitter-pattered off the wall.

'I don't know what you're worried about anyhow.'

'What'd I just tell you, madam?'

'I'll be surprised if they've got the wireless up here, never mind your TV.' Janice dunked the ginger snap in her coffee cup. She tried biting it. No, it was impossible.

'I've tried it. They're still stoatin'.' There was no reply from the overhead bunk. 'D'you hear what I said, Mr Clockerty? I said, I'll be surprised if they've even got the wireless up in – where is it we're goin' again?'

'Buckie, Miss Toner.' Eddie closed his eyes. For some reason he had a foreboding about Buckie.

★

'Good morning, good morning, good morning...,' chirruped the DJ in the cowboy shirt and kilt.

Danny glanced across the table at Bomba, whose phizog was the exact shade of an unsliced avocado. This was all they needed, he thought.

'You're tuned to Radio Buckie on 229 metres on the medium waveband....' MacAteer and McGlone winced as the heavy metal strathspey that identified the station ripped through their headsets. 'And I'm joined in the studio, as promised, by two great mates of mine....' Danny looked around to see who he was talking about '... Danny and Bambi!' The DJ punched up the fanfare jingle.

Dennis, who was propping up one of the partition walls, lowered his *Rolling Stone* and put the DJ straight.

'Like I say, Danny and *Bomba*....' The DJ acknowledged his blunder with a toothy grin into the mike. 'From the legendary showband, the Majestics.' Up fanfare.

Dennis held on to his temper and leaned over the turntables. 'They arenae a "showband", Jim.'

'Six short minutes after the big hour of six here on the *Breakfast Show* ... your old pal, Lachie, with you through till eight.' The fingers boogie-woogied along the row of buttons.

Dennis leaned over the turntables. ''Scuse me, Hamish, they arenae a....'

The DJ held up a hand for quiet. 'As we all know....' He had swapped his salty delivery for his Mr Sincerity voice. 'Danny's brother Jazza was recently taken from us in a horrendous road accident....'

Danny lowered his head to the table. Was nothing sacred to this dunce?

'So it's an especially warm Radio Buckie welcome to the band's latest signing for braving the elements to be with us on the phone-in this filthy morning.'

Too right, thought Danny. He and Bomba had sunk twenty-seven pints between them the previous night, and this was the morning after to beat the lot.

'And I believe we have our first caller on the line. . . .' The DJ gave Mr Sincerity the elbow and hunched eagerly over his mike.

Danny cleared his throat in readiness and screwed a finger into Bomba's ribs.

★

Noreen buried her face in the hotel hand towel.

'Get that radio back on, Vincent.'

Vincent dived under the bedclothes and drew them up round his chin. His head was splitting.

'It's off and it's stayin' off.' He spat the words at his wife's dressing gown.

Noreen switched it back on and tapped her toothbrush on the washbasin to the beat of the Majestics' 'Rip It Up'. She was looking forward to the phone-in. Unlike her husband's, Noreen Diver's face did not betray her age. It didn't lie about it, either – the crow's feet at the corners of her eyes weren't all laughter lines.

Vincent threw back the covers, leaped out of bed and wrenched the radio off.

'Take a tellin', will you?' He did not dive back into bed this time, but lowered himself gingerly onto the mattress.

Noreen gave up and walked to the door.

'Where're you goin'?'

Noreen turned the handle. 'Mind your own damned business.' She jerked the door open.

Vincent sat up. 'Don't slam that door! I'm warnin' you . . . don't slam that door, Noreen.' After twenty-two years

of marriage Vincent Diver still found it difficult to gauge his wife's feelings. He couldn't tell if this was just a temporary huff or whether she really was angry.

Noreen borrowed the sneery tone that was her husband's hallmark. 'Don't slam the door, Noreen, *please*?'

Vincent's temples throbbed. 'Don't slam the door, Noreen.' He gritted his teeth and thought of Glenna still lying in that hospital ward. '. . . please?'

★

'All right, we seem to have lost that caller for the moment, but we do have another call on line four, I believe,' crackled the hideously breezy voice on the radio.

There was a loud bang from along the hotel corridor and Suzi gave a start. 'What was that?' She sat up in bed.

'Shhhhh.' Fud cupped a hand behind his ear and strained to make out what was going on.

'I think you might have your radio set too near the phone, caller. Hullo?' The DJ's voice was lost in the snowstorm of static.

There was a knock at the door. 'Are you there, Suzi?'

Fud got up. 'I'll get it.'

What did Noreen want? Suzi pondered, plumping up her pillow and propping the portable on it.

'I know fine well he's been seeing some little. . . .' Noreen's voice trailed off as she caught sight of the Majestics' bass player. 'Oh!'

Suzi was insulted and amused at one and the same time. 'Don't be daft – he just doesn't have a wireless in his room.' She made a space on the end of the bed for Noreen and turned the radio down.

Fud's voice was peeved: 'We might be missin' somethin'.'

Suzi grabbed the portable off the pillow and turned the volume up full blast. 'And flounders at sixty-two pence a pound' was what he was missing, right? Suzi switched the set off and studied Noreen's ashen face.

'Is Vincent still pretending to have these headaches of his?'

And as the hour of the phone-in came and went, Noreen introduced Suzi to the miserable tale of her life as a rock'n'roll widow.

★

The commercials came to an abrupt end and Danny watched the kilted cowpoke jam the cans back on over his baseball cap.

'And away we go … stick an 0542 in front of that phone-in number if you're unlucky enough to be calling from outside the Buckie area … and we have another caller….'

Yet another 'What colour socks d'you wear?' fan with more 10ps than brain cells, no doubt, thought Danny wearily.

'Hi, you're through to Danny and Bomba….'

'I'd like to ask Bomba MacAteer something.' The voice was young, female and local. Danny was beginning to wish he'd stayed in bed.

'And your name is?' Lachie's curiosity was at odds with his countenance. He tugged his cap over his eyes and suppressed another yawn.

'Do you remember the last time the Majestics played Buckie?'

Danny wondered if this telephone doll had any idea what she was asking. The drummer could barely recall what he'd been doing ten minutes back. Anyway, it was time he stuck a few words in himself. 'You've got him there, sweetheart … they were all zonked out of their skulls on them pre-war package tours.' Danny's reward for that piece of info was a MacAteer mitt clamped over his gub.

'Yeah, it was 19….' Bomba's bloodshot eyes swept the studio ceiling. There was a long pause, then the avocado complexion gave way to a rather off-putting pink. '…64!' he said, triumphantly. 'There was the Majestics, Billy J. Kramer and the Dakotas, Peter and Gordon….'

What were they getting, Danny wondered, the Domesday Book of Rock?

'Gene Pitney, the Allisons….'

Danny's heart sank. Not the Gene Pitney birthday cake story *again*?

Inexorably, Bomba droned on. 'I remember Pitney used to close the first half of the show with one of his road managers bringin' on this birthday cake for him….'

Danny was fairly certain the telephone doll had died of boredom by this time.

'He done that every night on that particular tour.' Bomba gave a short laugh. 'Accordin' to my calculations he should be about 549 by now!'

To Danny's astonishment the telephone doll came back on the line. 'Yeah, I'm looking at a photograph of you and my Mum and a whole bunch of other people, and my Mum's cutting some sort of cake. It looks as if it was taken on a liner….'

'That was a back room at the British Legion Hall, sweetheart.' Bomba beamed. 'Vincent's birthday party … that was dead gen, we all got absolutely….'

'So there you go,' interrupted Lachie, teeing up the next record. 'A young lady with a fascinating souvenir of the Majestics' very first visit to Radio Buckieland, and now for….'

'I haven't asked my question yet.'

'Oh-oh.' A fingerstab from the DJ produced canned raspberries. 'Big boo-boo!'

'Can you remember giving my Mum a pendant?'

Danny could tell from Bomba's expression that this telephone doll was fast becoming a pest.

'You had it engraved with "I'll Never Get Over You. All My Loving, Bomba."'

The MacAteer cheeks resumed their sickly avocado tinge.

'I've just found it among her things. D'you remember my Mum?'

To Danny's relief, Bomba took this as an opportune moment to remove his mitt from his mouth and wrap it around the business end of the DJ's microphone.

'Get her off the line or I'm walkin', pal.'

Lachie's reaction was surprisingly swift. 'Yes sirree, a very interesting blether about a piece of Majestics' memorabilia. Let's have another caller now ... hullo?'

'She died last Friday from cancer.'

The MacDonald Sisters' 'Eetle A Doo Veel' hit the airwaves while the demented DJ hunted for the phone-in cut-off button. Bomba ripped off his cans and struggled to his feet. His vegetable impressions now embraced blenched celery.

'You might be interested to know when I was born. Hullo?'

Bomba tottered across the studio. Dennis held the door open.

'It was 27 June 1965.' The telephone doll's voice followed them down the corridor of the converted fishmeal shed. 'Exactly nine months to the day after the Majestics' concert!'

★

The elderly stag raised its antlered head and, taking its cue from Landseer, proceeded to pose for the passengers of the two-coach diesel hauling itself up the glen on the last lap of its journey from Aberdeen to Elgin, the stopping-off point for Buckie in the far north-east.

Inside the second coach Janice ran a magenta fingernail down the TV listings in her newspaper till she came to *Rockin' Through the Rye*. She looked up to let Eddie know what time it was on and spotted a familiar face further up the compartment.

'Oh-oh! Don't turn round, Mr Clockerty, but guess who's on the train?' She spread the newspaper open and held it up in front of her face.

Eddie stiffened. 'It's not Mrs Clockerty, is it?' He was supposed to be attending a dungaree convention in Harrogate, one of the hundred or so excuses which Eddie handed to his wife to cover for his clandestine but curiously non-carnal relationship with his secretary.

'Don't be daft, it's *her*.' Janice peered cautiously round the edge of her shield. 'Vincent's girlfriend.'

Eddie turned to look. Janice was livid.

'Hi!' She waved and smiled, then, without moving her lips, said, 'She's comin' to sit beside us now!'

Eddie stood up and shot Janice an enquiring glance. He wondered what she was getting so het up about. Perfectly nice wee lassie.

Glenna struggled down the aisle, dumped a mound of plastic carrier bags on the table and squeezed past Eddie into the window seat. 'I thought I'd take Vincent up a wee surprise.' She blew the strands of hair out of her face and delved into one of the plastic bags. 'I've knitted him a lumber jacket.' She produced a great fluffy blue and pink bundle and placed it lovingly on the table.

Janice stuffed a fist into her mouth and turned away.

'That's er. ...' It wasn't often that Eddie was stumped.

Glenna held up the fluffy object. It was indeed vaguely garment-shaped, but the sleeves had obviously been designed with an orang-utan in mind.

'D'you think he'll like the toggles?' Glenna hadn't been all that sure about those herself. She fiddled with one of the horn fastenings running down the front of the cardigan.

'What d'you think, Miss Toner?' Eddie turned to his companion, but Janice was for the time being quite incapable of speech. Eddie watched her heaving shoulders for a moment then hurriedly carried on. 'I don't suppose you've got any more of these, have you?' He was wondering whether to mention Wee Tommy Cairns's hunt for handknits for his San Diego Misfits outlet. He picked up one of the lumber jacket sleeves. 'Of course, they'd have to have the shorter full-length arm.'

Janice collapsed sideways onto her seat and bit hard into her fist.

Glenna's lips trembled. She grabbed Vincent's present, stuffed it back into its bag and stood up. 'Mind your feet, will you!' She gathered up the rest of her luggage and tried to shove past.

Eddie was distraught. 'No, don't go. ...' He tried desperately to remember her name and looked pleadingly to Janice, who mouthed something across the table top. Eddie stepped into the aisle and called after the tiny figure, 'Hold on a second, Glynis.'

She swung round, eyes blazing, and set the record straight as to her nomenclature.

A chastened Eddie shrivelled back into his seat and glowered at Janice. 'I sometimes wonder what gets into you, ya bism.'

Whatever it was that got into Janice got into her again, and heads turned as her derisive chortling echoed the entire length of the train.

★

'What if the haddock's finished?'

'Then I'll have the smokies.' Suzi set off along the corridor, towel round her neck, while Danny headed for the stairs. He didn't know how she could have any truck with a bathtub ... he certainly couldn't.

'Plenty of buttered toast, put the tea under the cosy, and don't touch my porridge.'

'Yes, Mummy Bear.'

He tripped lightly down the stairs and bebopped into the hotel dining room. Preparing himself for some leg-pulling about visiting the Kettles Suite at that ungodly hour of the morning, he found himself disappointed. Fud and Bomba were in tandem at one table, Vincent, solo, at another. Fud was the only one who looked up.

'You still havenae told us how come you walked off the radio show.' He waved his fork in Danny's direction, then shovelled a large piece of Arbroath smokie onto it. 'All the DJ would say was the switchboard was jammed.'

Danny had a look at Bomba, sitting there staring at the wallpaper with unseeing eyes.

'I knew that couldnae be true,' continued Fud.

Thank you, the bass player.

'Mornin', Vincent.' Danny bypassed the Diver table en route for the kitchen. Boy, was he starving. 'The wife had her breakfast, aye?'

Vincent kept his eyeballs riveted to his tabloid. 'She's washin' a coupla shirts for us.' He turned to page four and his lips started to move again.

Danny couldn't help wishing that somebody would do *his* laundry. 'Hullo?' He popped his head round the kitchen door.

'You want to get that burd of yours to do likewise,' came a disembodied voice from behind him.

Just what I was thinking, Vincent, murmured Danny to himself.

Fud slid Bomba's untouched smokies across the table and dolloped half a bottle of tomato sauce all over them. 'I hate to tell you, Danny Boy, but I think the kitchen staff's took a powder. We seen the wee wumman goin' out with her coat on, didn't we, Bomba?'

Danny let out a low groan while Bomba carried on counting the gravy stains on the wallpaper. ...

Upstairs, Suzi rapped her knuckles on the bathroom door. 'D'you think you could get a move on in there?' Lending a sympathetic ear to the Divers' diverse marital

problems before sun-up had caused her to work up a considerable appetite. Damn. She could hear the taps still running. Whoever was in there wasn't coming out yet. Just as she thought to go in search of another bathroom she realised that her slippers felt damp. She looked down, puzzled.

'Oh, my God....' She banged on the door with her fists.

The puddle on the landing carpet was getting bigger by the second. Suzi belted for the stairs at breakneck speed. McGlone might be useless at most things, but he stood a better chance of breaking down that bathroom door than she did....

'Danny!'

Aw, no. He tucked the plate of ketchup-covered smokies he'd got from Fud under the tablecloth.

'I'm not here, Kettles.'

Suzi tore into the dining room and seized him by the shoulder pads. 'Come quick, I need you!'

Could it not wait till he'd scoffed his fish, Danny pleaded.

'Get a move on, McGlone. I need you *now*!'

He flashed his 'I've had this problem with dolls all my days' smile at his fellow band members, and allowed himself to be dragged towards the door.

Suzi's face was serious. 'How can you talk about stuffing your face when there could be somebody up there drowning!'

Somebody up there what?

'C'mon, dummy! ...'

'Pretty obvious who wears the pants in that set-up.' Vincent flicked through his news comic till he came to the TV page. 'If Noreen spoke to me like that I'd lamp her one.'

Fud stopped chewing and looked across at Bomba. 'Did you hear that?'

Bomba was mulling over what Dennis had said in the Transit about paternity suits, retroactive child maintenance payments, newspaper reports, breaking the news to Christine...*and* to Diver. After all his threats to the guitar player about the way he'd been carrying on, *he* could expect no quarter....

'What?' Bomba dragged himself away from wallpaper study.

Fud swallowed his half-chewed smokie lump. 'D'you hear what he just said?'

'Who said?' Bomba tried to unscramble his brain.

'Forget it.'

Bomba shrugged and went back to staring out the wallpaper. Save for the steady chomping of Fud's jaws a gloomy silence descended once more....

The bathroom lock gave way at the second hefty shove from one of Big Jazza's size fourteens. Danny didn't know what he was expecting to see, but when it turned out to be Noreen sitting on the toilet in her dressing gown with her head lying against the cistern, eyes shut and mouth hanging open, he had to admit to himself that he felt a bit queasified. Three of Vincent's good shirts were floating about in the overflowing tub.

Suzi rushed forward and started shaking Noreen like a rag doll. An empty bottle of pills hit the lino.

Danny turned off the taps and pulled out the shirt sleeve that was blocking the overflow. It was a real dilemma, he found himself thinking. What should he phone first, the ambulance or the launderette?

★

It was very kind of Glenna to let them share her transport. Eddie was at some pains to acknowledge his and Miss Toner's indebtedness as all three squashed themselves and their luggage into the back of the taxi for the longish haul from Elgin.

'I can't think how else we would've got there. . . .' A row of sweat beads broke out on Eddie's brow. What was her name again? '. . . Glenda.' Phew. Thank God he'd remembered.

He looked to his left. 'Right, Miss Toner?'

Janice pressed her tongue into the middle of the wad of gum and blew a big pink bubble towards Eddie's face.

★

'Did Danny tell you what happened?' Suzi's voice was strained.

With a certain revulsion Danny watched Dennis press a handful of dry bran flakes into his maw.

'Didnae have to tell us,' the roadie replied, spraying the diners with a fine khaki dust. 'I've just been into the kitchen.' He lumbered to the door. 'Did you not get yours either?' Without waiting for an answer, he left.

Suzi goggled. 'A woman tries to kill herself,' she shouted at his back, 'and not one of you geeks bats an eyelid.' Angrily, she stood up.

Danny noticed she'd changed out of her pyjamas – and just as he was about to suggest they went upstairs for a 'snooze' too.

Suzi was at the dining room door before she spoke. 'This. . . .' She hesitated.

Is Your Life, Danny McGlone, no? No, it was worse than that.

'This is the last stop on my itinerary. Tomorrow I'm off.'

His jaw dropped. If the table hadn't been in the way it would have bounced off the linoleum. Tomorrow she was *what*?

'No, don't go . . . I love you, Suzi.'

They both looked up at the ornamental light fitting.

'I love you.' There it was again.

Suzi stood there stunned. Danny even more so. The only time he'd ever said that to anybody before was to his dead tortoise.

'Say that again, McGlone.'

He swallowed hard. He wasn't sure that he could. 'I . . . love . . . you.'

She put her head to one side. There was a long pause. 'No, even at a third hearing it's still got a distinctly bogus ring to it.'

Danny heard a croaking noise coming out of his throat. Suzi leaned against the door frame.

'Look, can we discuss this some other time? I'm going out to get some toothpaste.' She flung her jacket over her shoulder.

That put everything into perspective for Danny. A guy just admits to being crazy about a doll, and she's going out to buy toothpaste?

'Come back here, dammit!' He stood up and shouted.

Suzi spun round, the famous sangfroid gone. 'What is it *now*?'

Danny was just conscious of his lips forming the words: 'Don't get the stripey stuff – it stings my gums.'

★

The two brothers-in-law stood on the front steps of the hospital and waited. Vincent flicked his fag end at the No Smoking sign on the glass doors. As far as he was concerned *all* the MacAteers were nutters.

'What kinda drip?' He was still smarting from the news that Noreen had asked to see Bomba and not him.

'I don't know what kinda drip. Did you not ask the quack?' Bomba placed his heel on the still smouldering fag end and ground it into the concrete step.

Vincent thrust his fists into the pockets of his jeans and shivered. '*I* never got to see her, *I* never knew she was on a drip – so how could *I* ask the quack?'

Bomba stood on tiptoe and squinted along the street. 'S'that the wagon?' A fish truck hove into view.

'You sure you gave Dennis the right directions on the phone?' Vincent adjusted the flame control on the lighter he'd got from Glenna and tried again to light a fresh cigarette.

'I thought it was you that phoned?' Bomba lowered himself back onto his heels.

Vincent took the unlit Gitane from his mouth. A piece of his lip came with it. 'When would I get the chance to phone? I was discussin' Noreen's condition with her medical adviser, ya nitwit!' He could have qualified the statement by adding 'psychiatric', but he left it ambiguous.

'And I was discussin' possible grounds for divorce with your wife and my sister, so how the hell was *I* supposed to phone?' Bomba fired the salvo straight into Vincent's mug at close range.

Vincent wiped the spittle off and barged through the double doors, only to reappear immediately.

'What d'you mean "possible grounds for divorce"? What possible "possible grounds" could there possibly be!'

★

Suzi stood upright with some difficulty and started brushing her teeth.

Hiring a boat for an hour was Danny's brainwave for getting her on her own so he could pressurise her into reconsidering her decision to quit that other ship . . . the one that was sinking.

A skua peeled off from the motley bunch of seabirds circling overhead to dive-bomb the skiff, and Danny called to Suzi to let it have the toothpaste . . . he didn't fancy having his eyeballs plucked out of his head and fed to its young over a 75p tube of Mentadent P. A lobster boat putt-putted past on the port side and set them bobbing up and down in its swell. Danny placed a hand over his mouth. His phone-in hangover was getting worse. He

ordered Suzi to sit down and put the wireless on. Since losing both oars only minutes after setting sail from the pier there wasn't all that much to do but listen to a little music and wait for the tide to turn in their favour.

'You'll buff all the enamel off your wallies. Sit down and put the wireless on, I said!'

Suzi squatted obligingly in the bilges and stuck the portable on her head. She grinned at Danny.

That was what he was going to miss above all ... her impish sense of fun.

Danny leaned over the side and returned a partially digested smokie to the deep.

★

The Transit pulled up in front of the hotel and Vincent and Bomba got out.

Across the street, a young woman with blonde hair drew back into the shadows. She looked down at the large publicity photograph in her hand. That was him, the bastard. She stabbed the point of the switchblade into the middle of the picture and ripped it viciously across.

Dennis slammed the van door and followed the drummer and guitar player into the hotel.

The blonde released the catch on the knife, stuffed the mangled picture into her pocket and set off across the street. The wind off the Firth caught her coat and transformed her into an avenging angel.

The Majestics' guitar player closed the bedroom door and laid his head against the panel. He felt the thump-thump travel through the woodwork, run up his arm and back into his head to provide a throbbing quadrophonic effect. He was in a nightmare.

He opened his eyes and found himself staring at a blue and pink bundle on one of the beds. He closed his eyes. He was in the wrong room. He turned to leave.

'Boo!'

'*Aaaaaaaargh!*' Vincent spun round and fell back against the door, his fingernails clawing at the paint. It really was a nightmare.

As he watched Glenna rise up from the well between the beds he punched his fists into his eye sockets. Glenna climbed over the nearer bed and buried her face in the scuffed leather folds of his jerkin.

'Hullo, Daddy.' Glenna wrapped her arms around him and giggled.

Vincent went cold. ' "Daddy"?'

'I told Reception I was your daughter.'

He felt her warm lips on his throat. 'Did Reception tell you what happened to "Mummy"?'

Glenna gave a delighted squeak when she heard the news. So he had kept his promise. She squeezed him as tight as she could.

Vincent's eyes wandered to the bed and the blue and pink bundle. . . . 'What's *that*?'

Glenna gave another squeak. She knew he'd like it.

The malevolent trolls inside Vincent's skull finished their teabreak and picked up their sledgehammers again.

'It brings out the colour of your eyes.' Vincent's arms were forced down the four-foot-long woolly tubes.

Glenna stood back, happy. All that baby wool hadn't gone to waste after all.

'I trust that's doin' you a lot of good – it's made me feel very off-colour.' Dennis was appalled. Three quid for a big Courvoisier and a Pepsi was steep by any standards.

Bomba curled his fist round the brandy goblet. 'Talkin' about off-colour, look what's just strolled in.'

Dennis stole a look. The Pepsi came screaming straight down his nostrils.

'You guys okay, aye?' Vincent swaggered up to the bar and tried to light his Marlboro. 'Bacardi and Babycham, pal.' He rolled the sleeve of the lumber jacket up and had another go with the duff lighter.

Dennis crouched behind Bomba's back and crossed his legs.

Bomba's face was impassive. 'Dig the outfit, Vinnie. New, is it?' He tried to work out what the toggles were for.

'It's a present.' Vincent scrutinised the drummer's face for the slightest hint of a send-up. He caught sight of Glenna hovering uncertainly at the door. 'Over here, doll.' He waved a fluffy sleeve.

Bomba's nose twitched violently.

The balding barman placed the Bacardi and Babycham on the counter. He took in the lumber jacket but passed no comment.

'And what's for the young lady?' He gave Glenna a sympathetic smile.

Vincent's hackles went up. '*That's* for the young lady.' He thrust the drink into Glenna's hand and shoved her roughly towards the banquettes. 'I'm havin' a pint.'

Dennis doubled up with suppressed laughter and his head hit the bar-top.

Vincent could take no more. 'Stop starin' at us!'

Bomba hadn't been staring – he'd still been trying to fathom out what the toggles were for. 'Are they for keepin' the flies off?'

★

Vincent turned beetroot.

Janice entered the bar, took one look and turned turtle. Eddie caught one of her flippers.

'He's got it on!' Janice clutched at her middle.

Eddie was mystified. Who'd got what on?

'Shuttup, he'll hear you!'

'Over here, Eddie.' Bomba waved his glass.

Vincent glowered at Glenna. She hadn't told him *he* was here.

Eddie dragged the squirming Miss Toner across to the bar. 'What's everyone having?' He tried not to look at the Majestics' guitarist.

Vincent stood his ground while the shoulders around him heaved.

'Goin' to get us a packet of them wee cheesy what-d'you-me-callits?'

Vincent waved away Glenna's request with an angry gesture, then cursed his stupidity as he found his sleeve dangling around his kneecaps. That finished off Dennis. Janice held on to Eddie. Bomba stuck his face in the ice bucket.

No one paid any heed to the blonde-haired young woman who stood framed in the doorway. She took three paces into the room.

'Hullo ... Daddy.'

Bomba froze.

A chill descended on the bar. The hilarity evaporated. All eyes turned. There was a flash of steel, a scream. . . .

Vengeance is mine, saith the telephone doll.

The dying notes of 'The Finger of Suspicion' mingled with the cries of the herring gulls swooping low over the water before Lachie's strident tones broke in and destroyed the magic of the moment. 'The late, great Dickie Valentine there ... and while that superannuated number was assaulting your eardrums, we here at well-below-average Radio Buckie were in receipt of a –' chorus of whoops, cheers and flugelhorns '– world exclusive!'

Danny couldn't help remarking, as they drifted aimlessly about the harbour, that Lachie hadn't improved one jot since the *Breakfast Show*. A world exclusive on what ... the going rate on a cran of haddies?

'... on the stabbing incident at the Majestics' hotel right here in wonderful downtown Buckie!'

Suzi and Danny sat bolt upright in the bilges.

'More about that from George Alexander Nesbitt in our News Round-up at five....'

Suzi was the colour of death.

'And here to help take us up to the witching hour, Robert Walden Cassotto, a.k.a. Bobby Darin, and "Mack the Knife".'

Losing the oars had been hilarious at the time, but neither Suzi nor he was laughing too heartily now, Danny noted. He issued the order to paddle and dipped his mitts into the briny.

★

Fud O'Donnell bore his chagrin stoically, like a man who had missed out on most things and would go on missing out. Still, he was slightly peeved at having been caught napping while the stabbing was in progress.

'My legs went from under us, I don't mind tellin' you.' Dennis sat back and mopped his brow with a denim handkerchief. 'The bloody blade was about this size.' He spread his hands about three feet apart.

Fud looked a trifle sceptical.

Eddie stretched out a trembling hand. 'I'm not worth a button now.'

'She really *is* his daughter, then?' The bass player was now in a sulk. He'd been to the bar to have a shufti, but the bloodstains had been sponged off the wallpaper.

'Accordin' to the polis. They've still to check it out with the records, but you could tell a mile off.' The roadie turned to Eddie for support. 'Same sleekit look about the eyes, right?'

They all looked up as Bomba wandered into the dining room. He appeared grave and contemplative.

Dennis pulled over another chair. 'I'm sayin' to Francis, you could tell straight away it was Vincent's big lassie.'

The Majestics' drummer sat down and took the fake gold pendant from his pocket. He read the engraving again: 'I'll Never Get Over You. All My Loving, Bomba.... How many other dolls d'you suppose he gave one of these to?'

Eddie took hold of the pendant and dangled it between his fingers. 'I seem to recall he had some done with "All My Loving, Eddie" on them.' His mouth turned down at the corners. 'I'd always presumed that was meant to be Eddie Cochran, but now I'm not so sure....'

Bomba took the pendant back and snapped the chain. He had a good mind to go up that hospital and stick a knife in Diver himself.

★

'I'm still going home tomorrow ... as long as you realise that, McGlone.'

Danny attempted a smile. 'Sure, Kettles.'

Eddie had booked them into the biggest bingo hall in Buckie, and Danny was determined to put a brave face on things. It hadn't helped that the big board of numbers behind the band had lit up the instant he'd hit the introductory chord to 'Love Is Strange' and some wag in the stalls had bawled out 'House!', but Danny had managed somehow to prevent his voice from cracking too noticeably right through the first four numbers. It wasn't only love that was strange, he thought ... one of the band should get stabbed every day. It was the biggest crowd the Majestics had had since the tour kicked off in Methil. His eyes wandered over the packed house. Ghouls, that's what they were. Bloody ghouls. As Suzi bounced towards the front of the stage and rocked into an old Buddy Knox number Danny's thoughts strayed to Vincent and Noreen. It was ironic them ending up sharing the same cottage hospital together. Then again, life was full of little surprises. His only wish was that life would surprise them all again and prevent Kettles from heading back to Glasgow. Fat chance, he thought....

The ghouls put their hands together and howled their appreciation. Seldom if ever had the Majestics gone down so well. Danny felt ill. Here they were, he thought, the toast of the north-east – and this dumb doll has to go and blow it. As they trooped back on for their third encore Danny remembered that they were missing *Rockin' Through the Rye*, the TV event of the decade ... what the hell, he thought, looking longingly at Suzi, just so long as he could be with the woman he loved before the dozy cow vamoosed. Little could Danny know that at that precise moment the continuity announcer at Broadcasting House was apologising to viewers for the last-minute cancellation of the documentary and its consequent substitution by a rerun of half an hour's worth of gardening hints on mealy bug eradication.

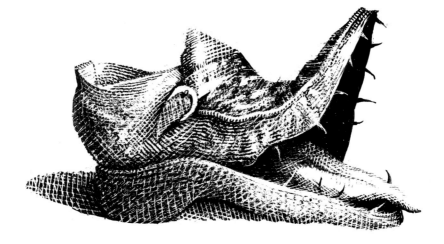

Love Hurts

The breeze coming off the Clyde had already run out of puff by the time it arrived in the city centre and set the chip pokes skittering along the gutters in a desultory dance. A scabby cat wolfed down the remains of a battered haddock from a week-old *Glasgow Evening Times*, on the front page of which a grinning Vincent Diver was featured, strangely at odds with the headlines above and below his photograph: 'Majestic Knifed in Buckie' and 'Bedside Vigil for Rock Star Vince (44) as Daughter Is Remanded'. Eddie had thought it expedient to knock a few years off Vincent's age when supplying the reporter with the photo.

The sudden crash of drums from a basement ventilator sent the cat rocketing sideways, its Sunday breakfast abandoned, its back arched and its eyes sticking out like two yellow bools.

Inside the subterranean studio the Majestics' lead guitarist counted off the beats, then launched headlong into the opening lines of 'You're Sixteen', the old Johnny Burnette smash. Despite its being the nineteenth take, Vincent Diver was still giving it everything he had, which was not an inconsiderable amount even though he was hampered by his surgical collar and with having to stretch from his wheelchair to reach the overhead mike.

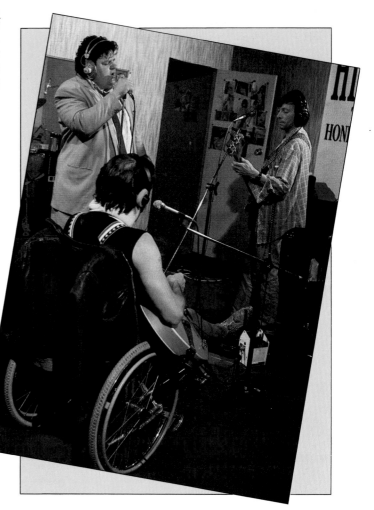

Dennis sat beside the bespectacled young engineer in the control booth and watched the tapes roll, a look of consternation on his bovine features. 'I'm not sure about you, pal, but it still sounds to me like they're vocalisin' through about forty layers of burlap.'

The engineer, inured to insult after twenty-seven hours in the roadie's company, made constant adjustments to the various faders and channel slides on the desk in front of him.

Dennis stole a peek at his annotated chart. He waited till the engineer had removed his glasses to wipe the condensation off them, then reached forward and gave one of the knobs a sharp twist.

★

While the Majestics were having their eardrums syringed in one part of the city, in another more salubrious area Suzi Kettles was happily settling down with the *Observer* Review and humming along with Billie Holiday on the Dansette.

The doorbell rang for a second time.

Suzi licked the marmalade off the burnt crust and placed the crust carefully on top of the pillow. She swung her legs out of bed.

The doorbell rang yet again.

'I'm coming.' The hunt for one missing slipper was abandoned and Suzi limped along the unheated hallway.

'I thought I gave you a key, ya big....' The 'dumplin'' died on her lips as she found herself staring into the too-tanned-to-be-true face of her estranged dentist husband, Stuart Gordon Inverrarity.

Before she could stop him, the diminutive Inverrarity had shoved her aside and was making his way up the hall, kicking doors open as he went.

'Hey, stop that!' Suzi ran after him and caught hold of his jacket.

'Three weeks, Suzi....' He crossed to the bathroom and looked inside. 'I telephoned, I asked around....'

'You can't barge in here and....'

The back-handed blow was almost casual. It caught her cheekbone and sent her thudding into the wall.

'Where've you been for the past three weeks?' he demanded menacingly.

As Inverrarity took hold of her arm and twisted it behind her back Suzi screamed with pain.

'You've been off screwing around, haven't you?' He grabbed her hair and forced her head back. 'Haven't you, you bitch!'

'No, please, Stuart ... please, *oooooooow*!'

The next blow sent her reeling drunkenly over the back of the couch. She lay there winded, tasting the blood on her tongue. Then he was on top of her, pinning her hands

behind her head. He shoved his mouth brutally onto hers. Her stomach heaved. She felt him press himself against her.

'That's all you were ever good for, wasn't it, you cow!' His breath smelt foul.

Suzi only had to raise her head an inch to sink her teeth into his nose. She felt his body buck, but she held on till she tasted his blood mingled with her own.

'*Aaaaaaaaaaaaaaooooooooooooowwwww!*' Inverrarity fell backwards onto the floor, clutching his face in agony.

Suzi spat at the writhing figure.

'You cow!' The dentist sat up and stared at his bloody palms.

Suzi made a dive for the phone, but before she could even dial the first digit of the number Danny had given her the phone was sent crashing across the room.

'You talk to anybody and it's the last thing you do, d'you hear?'

Suzi felt as if the top of her skull was coming off as Inverrarity repeated the hair-pulling trick.

'D'you hear?'

Desperately, she moaned, 'Danny! ...'

★

Eddie Clockerty sat behind his desk, an unlit half Corona firmly clenched between his dentures and the Pavilion Theatre seating plan spread in front of him. At his left hand was an ancient adding machine, at his right a cup of instant soup. It was unusual for the Clockerty Enterprises HQ to be fully manned on a Sunday, but exceptional times required exceptional measures. While Eddie provided fodder for the adding machine, Janice was under orders to leaf through the Sundays and ring any mention of Vincent's 'accident' – whether in the gossip or showbiz columns – in red. Knowing her task to be fruitless – after all, it hadn't been Frank Sinatra who'd got chibbed in Buckie – Janice had spent most of the morning digesting a fashion feature on the re-emergence of Tommy Nutter and was about to tackle the book reviews when something caught her eye....

'Aw, God, listen to this, Mr Clockerty....'

'Just a second, Janice.' Eddie cranked the handle of the adding machine and erased the decimal point on the resultant total.

'Postponed from a fortnight ago due to "technical problems", this fascinating glimpse under the flat stone of rock'n'roll....'

Flat stone of rock'n'roll? What was the stupid girl on about now? Eddie pencilled in another nought at the end of the row of figures.

Janice folded the paper over. '... has been rescheduled to coincide with the live appearance in Glasgow at the climax of their less than earth-shattering Silver Jubilee Tour by the Majestics....'

There was a crash. Janice cast a disapproving glance at the adding machine sitting in the waste-paper basket into which Eddie had swept it.

'We were always working to hairline tolerances, Miss Toner.'

★

Danny tried to recall the last time he'd been this tired, but fell asleep in the process. He woke up with a jerk and looked at his watch. Thirty-two hours he'd been locked in the bowels of the earth with the survivors from another century, trying to hack an LP out of a solid hunk of acetate. His vocal cords were in tatters – even the nodes on his vocal cords were in tatters. His shoulders ached. His eyeballs felt like they'd been cooked. Even the spaces between his toes were hurting. He saw Diver sailing past in his cripple carriage, a manic grin floating above the surgical collar. Whatever it was he'd got, thought Danny, Vincent could keep away from him – *he* didn't want it. Then everything went black, except he could still hear somebody's stupid voice.

'We'll need some horns and a bunch of chicks for the doo-wah wahs.'

A bunch of chicks for the whats? A warm tailwind ruffled Danny's hairdo as the invalid chair sped past with its driver shouting out for O'Donnell to give him a shove to the phone – he wanted to ring Noreen before she went to the launderette or some rubbish. Then Danny slid back into a dwam and started dreaming about himself and Suzi again, only this time he found that the giant tortoise with the snorkel didn't get to its pins and start shooting its mouth off when the priest said, 'If anyone knows of any impediment to this marriage....'

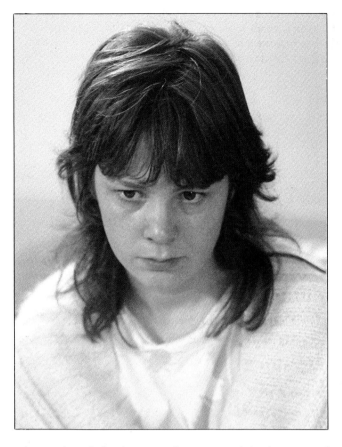

Glenna shrank further into the corner of the lounge and drew the blue, pink and bloodstained lumber jacket tighter around her narrow shoulders. She scrunched her knees up to her chin and squeezed the small rubber doll with the blank, bitten face that was a relic from her childhood. She could see the doctor's face and hear his lies going round and round in her head . . . phantom pregnancy . . . phantom pregnancy. . . . Liar! She gave an involuntary shudder and hurled the doll violently across the room. It lay with its blank, bitten face against the fender. Bloody liar! Glenna stabbed out her cigarette on the carpet and reached for another one amongst the debris spread all around her. Her hand shook but her gaze was steady, unblinking, as she lit the crumpled cigarette. The baby had died . . . it had died.

If she heard the telephone ringing she gave no sign. Nobody ever called any more, she thought. Not Vincent, not anybody. It was as if she was dead. Along with the baby. . . .

★

'Dozy bitch!' Vincent slammed the payphone down. Having got no joy from either house he was in no mood for Fud's supposition that 'the girls' had gone off to the launderette together. Then he had a sudden inspiration. The only way to get on top – a come-back – was to rework the original hit of 1962. As he dialled the Clockerty Enterprises number he enquired, 'How good a chanteuse is this burd of Danny Boy's?' Having Suzi as a lowly back-up singer would soon put that jumped-up doll in her place, thought Vincent.

The bass player baulked. So it wasn't a wind-up – they really were going to attempt a rework of their number seven single.

'Don't look so surprised – we can do it again if we get the right line-up. . . . Hullo, Eddie? Hold on to your hat and cop this for an idea. . . .'

Fud O'Donnell gazed up at the flaking ceiling and groaned.

The Morris Minor Estate turned into the tree-lined avenue and crawled past the rows of semi-detached villas. The health visitor behind the wheel held up a letter and checked the house numbers against the address at the top. The car drew to a halt.

Although it was a Sunday Noreen had put on her uniform because in a funny way she regarded this as a 'health' visit. She wasn't one to stand idly by and watch her marriage perish without having one shot at resuscitation. She would have been a liar if she'd said she hadn't wondered who the anonymous letter writer might be, but neither had she agonised over his or her identity. Well, hers . . . her identity. Weren't all anonymous letter writers female? Or was that poison pens? No matter, she was here now. She looped a finger through the string of the cake box on the passenger seat and opened the car door.

★

Danny stuffed the 10p piece back in his pocket and wondered why he'd bothered. Every time he tried the number it was engaged. He'd known dolls to be on the telephone for three days at a stretch, he recalled in frustration, and Kettles was obviously no exception. He repaired to the studio with a light head and a heavy heart. Supposing she'd taken the phone off the hook because she just didn't want to talk to him, he thought, exhaustion aggravating the paranoia he was already prey to. He didn't want to think about that. He checked to see if he still had the key to her apartment and discovered it languishing amongst the oose in his back pocket. Maybe he'd do best to make a personal call on her? Yeah, that was it. He yawned. The noise of his jaw cracking was the most musical sound he'd heard in the past couple of hours.

'If she doesnae cut it I'll give you the nod and you can bump her, okay?' Diver did a three-point turn in his wheelchair and ran over his brother-in-law's foot. Bomba didn't even stir.

Cut what – bump who, Danny pondered vaguely. It was several minutes before it dawned on him that he was talking about doo-wah wahs and Suzi. Who was this joker trying to kid, he thought angrily, now very wide awake indeed.

'Tell her she'll get twenty notes for the session – I've cleared it with Eddie.' Diver had quit whirling dervish-style and was sitting looking at Danny as if he was expecting an answer.

He got his answer, but not the one he was expecting. Doo-wah wahs! What an insult to the doll. 'She gave you a right showin' up on them gigs you never turned up for.'

Danny thought Vincent was going to burst a blood vessel.

'Never turned up for? *Never* . . .,' he screamed. 'The reasons I never "turned up", McGlone, were, number one, I was involved in a car smash, and numbers two and three, I was lyin' flat on my back in intensive care with stab wounds to my throat and testicles!'

What kind of a lame excuse d'you call that, murmured Danny almost, but not quite, to himself.

Noreen moved to another part of the flower bed and knocked on the window again. She could quite plainly see a pair of feet sticking out from behind the sofa.

'I tried the front door,' she called. 'Hullo?'

The feet gave a little twitch.

Noreen took off her glove and rapped her knuckles against the glass. 'I can see your feet sticking out ... *hullo?*'

The feet disappeared. A few seconds later a small face, like a child's, appeared above the sofa.

Noreen held up the cake box.

The face closed its eyes and opened its mouth wide.

Noreen took a step back onto the grass. If anybody should be screaming it should be her. She didn't even like rum babas.

★

After two days in the Tombs anybody's voice would have been music to Danny's ears, but Suzi's sounded like Mozart, Little Richard and Clifton Chenier rolled into one. He could have lain on that sofa in her living room and listened to it till the cows came home, but he hankered after a glimpse at her flawless kisser to accompany it.

'Give me a second, Danny...,' she called from the bedroom.

What was it with dolls they needed about ten weeks to rub on a dab of rouge and spit into their mascara?

'Before I come in there's something I've got to tell you.'

What? That the place was a mess? He could see that.

'You know how you asked me a while back if there was anybody?'

Was anybody? Aw, yeah, a guy. He vaguely remembered.

'A guy ... d'you remember?'

He remembered, he remembered. He yawned but he remembered....

The next thing Danny knew he was being shaken violently and there were Suzi's features in big close-up ... except that he didn't recall the black eye and the sundry bruising around the jaw.

'His name's Inverrarity and he's a dentist. Oh, Danny, Danny....'

Then she started bubbling uncontrollably – Danny could feel the tears soaking right through his good shirt. He lifted up her chin, thinking he'd better have a gander at the damage ... she'd said something about a dentist.

Then he put the one question that seemed relevant. 'What was it, a wisdom tooth?'

★

Vincent jammed a hand over the payphone. His eyes were spinning in his head. He'd dialled the wrong number and nearly blown it! Then he pulled himself together. 'Aw, er ... hullo, Noreen....' He looked at Fud.

Fud looked back at him.

'You're back from the launderette then?' He gave the bass player a wink. Nerves of steel, eh? 'I rang you earlier on but you werenae there ... what?' Vincent listened.

Fud watched.

'No, I don't follow that. What d'you mean, "no, that's because I'm here"?' What was the dozy bitch talking about? 'I said, I rang you earlier but....' Vincent tore the telephone from his ear and rammed it against his chest. His eyeballs strafed the walls before fixing on Fud. 'She just asked me if I want to talk to Glenna!'

Fud shrugged. He did want to talk to Glenna, didn't he?

Vincent reached over and belted the bass player with the receiver.

★

'S. Gordon Inverrarity LDS.' Danny gave the brass plate a rub with his sleeve, but he knew the past couldn't be erased that easily. He felt strange, as if in a dream. Suzi was away down the street before he caught up with her. He still hadn't found out why she'd made a date with this psychopath husband of hers in the first place, so he put the question again.

'I broke the date.' She took off the dark glasses and jabbed them at her swollen face. 'Which is why he came looking for me, stupid.' She started to walk away again.

That was not what he'd asked her, Danny persevered.

'I had something to discuss with him.' She yanked her arm away.

Something, yeah – but what something? Getting back together, was that it?

'Yeah, I really missed getting my face punched in – what d'you think?'

Danny knew exactly what *he* thought, he said – he was getting made a right mug of. How come she'd never told him about this husband of hers before? And how come she was making secret rendezvous with him, even if she didn't turn up for them?

Danny's outburst seemed to catch her on the raw and she spun round in fury. Who the hell did he think he was, telling her who she could and who she couldn't meet?

Who indeed, thought the luckless Danny, overcome with self-pity. He was just the dope that slept in the bath and took her on tour and got kept in the dark about the dentist – who was *he* to tell her anything? 'I'll tell you this much, Kettles,' he shouted suddenly. 'I wish to God I was back in that scummy walk-up with the Funny Shoe Salesman – at least I knew where I was with him!'

With that he strode off angrily down the appropriately named Bath Street, punching walls and buildings as he passed. There were tons of dolls just dying to get their munchers into his torso. Tons of them, he shouted over his shoulder. But somehow, the stabbing pain from his battered knuckles couldn't quite eradicate the other pain he felt inside.

★

'So....' Sheena Fisher sat down, crossed her legs, wrapped her glossy lips around the straw and sucked. 'To what do we owe this unexpected pleasure?'

Danny didn't like to point out that the cocktail she was getting stove into at the Holiday Inn poolside was merely an aperitif – the 'unexpected pleasure' would come later ... after all, she was a woman of the world, right?

He was just about to toss the room key onto the table when she started telling him about how she'd just been talking to this big, big fan of his, which had Danny momentarily distracted from the main purpose of this little rendezvous. 'Jamie Abernethy,' she continued. 'He said you and he were at Art School together. Called you the Great White Hope of Scottish Art – said you'd made a terrific hit in New York.' She slowly uncrossed her legs, then even more slowly recrossed them. 'That can't be true, can it?'

Danny slowly uncrossed his eyes. Who wanted to be the Great White Hope of anything, never mind Scottish Art? It was racist for a kick-off, and contrived to demean both art and his ancestry. McGlone was an Irish name. He had not, however, spent that 10p on a phone call to invite Ms Fisher to a seminar on genealogy. To business, his inner voice told him. He chucked the room key across the table.

'You go up first, sweetheart. I'll be right at your back.' He didn't have all that much time – he had an album session to get back to.

'Pardon me?'

If she ever jacked in the telly, Danny thought, she could get a job in the theatre – no sweat.

'All right, we'll go up together.' He didn't mind, he told himself, as long as *she* didn't mind the paparazzi popping their flashbulbs at them as they stepped arm in arm into the elevator.

She sat where she was. Danny was perplexed. Maybe she needed another stiff one?

'Look, we both know why I'm here, Danny,' she said in a matter-of-fact way.

Thank God for that, he thought. He'd just started to think he might have to draw her a picture. He took the empty glass off her.

'If you want to discuss Friday night's transmission let's discuss it – only don't piss me around, okay?'

If he wanted to discuss *what*?

'C'mon, you saw the sneak in today's papers....'

Sneak? He'd never seen any sneak.

'It wasn't deliberate, I assure you ... it really was a snarl-up in telecine last time....' Her voice petered out. It was perfectly obvious from Danny's blank look that he hadn't the foggiest what she was on about. Then she began to get angry. 'So what *am* I doing here?'

She'd told Danny the next time he was in town to give her a ring – that's what she was doing there, he informed her. What'd she think he was, daft or something?

'My God, of all the maladroit seducers....' She uncrossed her legs in earnest this time and stood up. Just before she got to the street door she turned and delivered her parting shot: 'Now, if you'd been the Beast of Rock, Danny....' She left the rest unsaid and stomped outside into a taxi.

If he'd been the Beast of Rock, Danny thought savagely, he wouldn't have had to phone the likes of Ms Fisher. He could've kicked his own teeth in, thanks!

★

'D'you want me to ring round the mortuaries, Mr Clockerty?'

Eddie was in no mood for banter, least of all Miss Toner's. 'We're just waiting for one of our personnel, then we can make a start, lads.' He addressed the taller of the two sax players, the one without the hearing aid. The sax players carried on practising their Charlie Parker motets.

'Can we get restarted soon, Eddie?' Fud put the brake on Vincent's wheelchair and picked up his Rickenbacker. He was anxious to get home to Ivy and the kids.

'Just as soon as the squeezebox players arrive.' Eddie

pushed the Majestics' bass player to one side and called up to the control box, where Dennis the roadie was to be seen but not heard trying to persuade the engineer that spilt coffee wasn't all that injurious to the latest technology, surely to God?

Fud turned to Janice. 'Did he say "squeezebox players"?' What kind of backing for a rock'n'roll band was *that* meant to be?

But Janice was too fascinated watching Vincent Diver, whose throat wounds had reopened, deposit yet another yuckel of dark blood onto the lino to answer.

Through all this rammy Bomba MacAteer, secure behind his baffle boards, slept soundly and peacefully.

★

Noreen unloaded the last armful of clothing from the back of the Morris Minor and heaved it on top of the three-foot-high pile she'd made among the discarded wine bottles and rotting newspapers. She upended the petrol can, sprinkled paraffin over it all, and reached into her coat pocket for the box of matches. She felt a twinge of regret that she hadn't donated at least part of her husband's extensive wardrobe to one of the several charity shops she'd passed on her way to the piece of waste ground. But any residual guilt was assuaged by the satisfying *whoomp* as the match hit its target.

Noreen retreated a short distance and shielded her face against the heat. It was the first real warmth she'd experienced in over twenty years of marriage.

★

There was a crackle as the talkback facility came on. Everybody held their breath. Bomba, Fud and Danny hung on to Vincent's wheelchair ... the Saxophone Brothers held on to each other ... the Inverbervie Ceilidh Quintet, resplendent in full Highland regalia, linked arms. It was a tense moment.

Eddie's voice, hoarse with fatigue, croaked out: 'Thank you, boys and girls....'

You could've driven a line of Churchill tanks through the pause.

Another crackle.

'I'm told we have a record.'

Danny felt his knees buckle. Diver slumped in his chair, his tongue lolling. MacAteer fell back against his hi-hat. A ragged cheer went up. The clock showed 6.17 a.m., but nobody knew what day it was. The Majestics had their souvenir album in the can and their first single since '62. Danny's thoughts turned to Big Jazza. Wherever he was right then he must've felt proud. Very hot but very proud....

He waited till the studio had cleared before sitting down at the keyboards and picking out 'Love Hurts', fast becoming his Favourite Music of All Time. It wasn't that he fancied Janice or anything ... it was just that he knew she was sitting up in that control booth all on her ownio and here he was with the key to a twin-bedded room at the Holiday Inn and nobody to ease the pain. Danny sang the opening verse with real feeling. He embellished the piano accompaniment with baroque ornamentation. His eyes wandered towards the booth. 'Er...you up there, Janice?'

★

While Suzi Kettles sat in her singular apartment staring disconsolately at the mound of maternity benefit leaflets and quietly but sincerely cursing her fortune, herself and her estranged husband, Glenna McFadden sat up in bed in her unshared semi and joined Roy Orbison in wishing his baby sweet dreams. She was concentrating on getting her lipstick on. Maybe having a mirror would have helped, but Glenna didn't appear to mind. Anyway, she knew roughly where her lips were. And that's roughly where the lipstick went.

★

'You tried the Dental Hospital, I see?' Inverrarity commented, glancing down at the card his receptionist had brought in just before Danny walked into the surgery.

'Er... yeah, they didnae have a big enough pair of pliers, so they sent me down here.' Danny kept the handkerchief up to his face. He'd made up the bit about the Dental Hospital so she'd put him down for an emergency extraction. His feigned distress, however, turned to real angst as the dentist shut the surgery door and switched channels on the wall-mounted speakers. The piped jazz gave way to disco funk.

The necessary adjustments were made to the chair. This puncher-out of dolls wasn't at all what Danny'd imagined, with his Yankee-style short-sleeved smock and boyish grin. The original intention in Danny's mind had just been to batter his head off the floor and beat it, but he could hardly mete out such a cuffing to somebody who barely came up to his kneecaps, could he? He had to come up with something a little more sophisticated. But what? A severe talking-to, mused Danny, didn't strike him as a fitting enough punishment.

'Mrs Beattie tells me you've been chasing away all my other patients, Mr...?'

Too right he had, thought Danny. He didn't want any witnesses, did he?

'Now, why would a nice big chap like yourself want to do something like that, hmm?' Inverrarity motioned him to sit down.

And at that moment inspiration struck Danny. 'Because a nice big guy like myself doesn't go a bundle on wee dentists like you that get their rocks off from punchin' out dolls, that's why.' He grabbed a bunch of Yankee smock and shoved the dentist into his own chair. He was like a frightened bunny rabbit, Danny thought, almost feeling sorry for the guy. But then he remembered the damage to Suzi's physiognomy, and he reached up for the drill.

Glenna, a faraway smile on her face, walked slowly across the suspension bridge – the same bridge the Majestics' Transit had crossed en route for the Aberdeen gig several hours earlier – and stopped in the middle. The evening sun dipped behind the hills and left the cityscape etched in gold. It was the last sunset that Glenna was ever to see. During her slow fall, as in a soft-focus shot, towards the murky waters Glenna didn't call out or think of Vincent.

But, far away, Vincent was thinking of her. Or someone very like her. There were so many chicks like Glenna, it was hard to distinguish between them all.

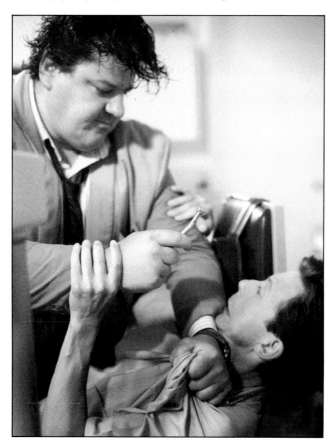

★

A-Wop Boppa Loo Bop, A-Wop Bam Boom...

'No, no, it's very nice ... I'm touched.' Vincent Diver stuck his crutches down the side of the chair and took hold of the wreath. He laid it with the rest of Glenna's belongings on the carpet.

Danny was glad he'd had the forethought to remove the robin redbreast. Not that there was anything intrinsically up with robin redbreasts, he assured himself. They just didn't look right on funeral wreaths, that was all.

The poor guy was clearly teetering on the brink of an emotional precipice, he thought. 'Best get it out, pal.' Danny was pretty sure he knew how Vincent was feeling. It was like a dam had got built in your chest, only you thought it was never going to burst. He felt in his pocket. Yeah, it was still there. Danny straightened its beak out before producing it. After all, Glenna might well have been partial to robins. His insight – or was it his sensitivity – seemed to be telling him something.

Danny watched in fascination as Diver's bottom lip started to go. The guitarist reached out a trembling hand and picked up the small brown ball. One of its legs fell off. Danny coughed loudly and turned his attention to a pile of snapshots spilling out of the deceased's toilet bag all over the carpet.

'That's one her and I had took up in Lossiemouth.' Diver bent down and picked up one of the snaps.

Danny glanced at it. Vincent and Glenna on the sands.

'Guy up our street used to have a pair of trunks identical to them.' Danny handed him back the snapshot – it's always difficult, he thought, knowing what to say in these circumstances.

They sat quietly for a while after that.

When Vincent did eventually speak his voice was cracked with emotion. 'You don't go out of your road to fall head over heels for a doll. It just happens....'

Danny thought about Suzi. 'Aye, one minute you're just an Ordinary Joe with ordinary, everyday wants and feelin's, then you bump into a broad ... next thing you know, you're a basket case ... cannae eat, cannae sleep ... all you want to do is be with them, look at them, touch them ... aw, God, I know exactly how you feel, Vinnie.'

Vincent's head snapped up. 'What'd you just say?'

Danny started to repeat the parable of the Ordinary Joe, but Vincent jerked up a hand. 'No, no, you called me "Vinnie".'

Danny was slightly perplexed. That was his name, wasn't it?

'Aye....' Vincent was on his feet now. 'But that's the first time you've ever called us it!' He swayed like a corn stalk in the breeze.

Danny urged him to get a grip ... it was hardly the Miracle at Lourdes.

Vincent, however, had difficulty containing himself. 'I know, I know. But d'you not see, Danny?'

Danny's perplexity turned to outright astonishment. For the first time ever the guitar player had used his name without sticking a derogatory 'Boy' on the end of it. He excused himself and got up to go to the toilet ... very bad for his image, thought Danny, for Diver to clock him with an overflowing tear duct.

He was not alone in harbouring such fears.

'What about *my* image?' Vincent yelped at Danny's retreating suit.

Danny swivelled and stared at the Majestics' guitarist. Vincent didn't have an image, did he?

Diver's craggy features set into a granite mask. A crevasse opened up in the granite. ' "The Iron Man of Scottish Rock", pal.'

Sorry?

' "The Iron Man of Scottish...." ' Vincent sniffed. ' "The Iron Man of...." ' He wiped his nose. ' "The Iron...." ' The granite started to crumble. 'Aw, Christ....' Vincent slumped back into his chair, his head buried in his hands. 'Aw, Christ....'

The dam was breached.

Eddie rubbed the green ring where the chunky links of the 'gold' identity bracelet were chafing his wrist and studied the faces of the Majestics' drummer and bass player sitting across the desk. It had taken a bit of work tracking the Kettles girl down since she'd abandoned her flat, and time was running out. The buzz of the internal telephone interrupted his thoughts.

'What is it, Janice? I'm in an emergency meeting....'

Bomba MacAteer came round the desk and leaned over Eddie's shoulder. 'You ... are an evil, connivin'....'

Eddie replaced the receiver. 'That's the souvenir pressings just arrived downstairs. Listen, Bomba....'

Bomba see-sawed across the carpet square. 'Okay, I've never liked the guy. I want to throw up when I'm in the same room as him. But for you to suggest bumpin' him off after twenty-five years and replacin' him with this ... this....'

Fud O'Donnell helped him out. 'Chick.'

'God almighty, Eddie!' Bomba gave the drinks cabinet a kick.

Eddie frowned. He'd obviously been too cryptic. 'No, no, you've got hold of the wrong end of the stick, Bomba son.' He picked up the external phone and dialled. 'I'm not talking about Vincent....' He tried to remember the extension number he was after. 'I'm talking about Danny Boy.'

Bomba stopped nursing his foot and looked up. 'Danny Boy?'

'I still haven't broached it with Miss Kettles yet – she could just as easy turn round and say ... hullo?' Eddie cranked his executive chair round and put his feet up on the desk. 'Yes, could I have a word with Sheena Fisher, please? It's a matter of some urgency, tell her.'

★

'I've still got the smell of her hair in my nostrils.'

As Danny passed Vincent a hanky he said bravely, 'You realise this joint's goin' to be jam-packed tomorrow night, don't you?' No, Danny didn't believe it either – he was just groping for some way to drag Vincent up from the bottom of the well.

It really was a pitiful sight, the Majestics' once proud guitar boss sitting there with the tattered lumber jacket hanging off one shoulder, its sleeves dangling over the chair like a couple of woolly pythons. Danny topped up Vincent's tea with another stiff tot from the whisky bottle and thought what he might wear for the climactic gig of the Silver Jubilee Tour at the Pavilion. The chocolate two-piece? The Bacofoil number? What did Vincent think?

'I'm thinkin' about Glenna.'

Sufferin' God in heaven.... Danny told him sharply that all the thinking in the world was not going to bring her back and would he kindly chuck it? He slurped another snort into Vincent's mug. 'That's your last, okay?'

Vincent raised the mug to his lips, then brought it back down again untouched. 'No, I don't think I can face it, Danny.'

It was pleasing to see Diver showing a modicum of restraint. After all, Danny reminded him, they did have a sound check shortly, and would Vincent like him to pour it down the cludgie?

But no. It was the Pavilion he couldn't face, he said, pouring the whisky straight down his neck.

The Iron Man of Scottish Rock not able to face it? If Danny got him talking, he reckoned, it might take his mind off the Munchkin. 'What're you givin' us?'

'I'm forty-eight next birthday, that's what I'm givin' you.' He held out the mug for a top-up. 'I'm shagged out

from sittin' hunkered up in a Transit van for the past six weeks kiddin' on I'm lovin' every minute of it.'

Vincent was not the only one, Danny assured him. He freshened the guitar player's drink.

'I'm fed up playin' the same old riffs to the same old riff-raff for the same old amount of washers in the same old dives....'

Danny lit up a fag and settled back.

'We havenae had a hit record since nineteen-forget-about-it and even that was a fix, so there's not much likelihood of us havin' another one.'

Danny said he couldn't have agreed more.

'I've had my skull split open, my musical competence questioned, my motor burnt out, my clobber destroyed by an arsonist.... I'm lumbered with two houses to pay for and no offspring that I know about except for a big lassie that turns out to be Jack the Ripper in high heels!'

Aye, that was unfortunate, Danny agreed. He blew a perfect smoke ring and watched it encircle one of Vincent's crutches.

'And as if that wasnae enough I've went and lost the one person in the world I ever cared two cents for ... aw, God....' His head fell into his lap.

It was getting too much for Danny. 'I'd go easy on the sauce if I was you, Vinnie,' he said, screwing the top back on the whisky bottle.

Vincent drew one of the lumber jacket sleeves across his streaming face. 'Don't "Vinnie" me, McGlone.' He struggled out of his chair. His voice was like a chicken getting drawn through a bandsaw. 'Who invited you to come strollin' in here in your manky footwear and....'

They both spotted the cigarette burns on the carpet at the same instant.

Danny looked around for somewhere to stub out his fag.

'Aw, God, look at this!' Diver cried.

Look at what?

'And this!' Diver swayed across the room, pointing out a whole load of singe marks with the end of his crutch. 'Christ, there's another one over there!'

'I'm sorry.'

'You're sorry? You're ...?'

For one terrible second Danny thought Vincent was going to open his skull with a crutch.

'It's too bloody late to be sorry now, isn't it?' The whisky mug shattered off the far wall. 'She's not here to give us a row for doin' that to the good carpet, is she!'

Danny's heart sank to the three-inch soles of his leopardskin loafers. He might've guessed the Munchkin would get herself into the act.

his voice dramatically. 'Miss Toner is quite unused to that sort of advance, as you can imagine.' He turned his head abruptly and signalled to the waiter. 'As for Sheena Fisher ... well....' Danny's drink-induced 'confession' concerning the Holiday Inn seduction attempt had provided Eddie with enough information, no matter how distorted he knew it to be, to lard his own revelations with all the innuendo required.

Suzi sat and seethed. When she did eventually speak it was in an uncharacteristically loud voice. 'When d'you want me to start?'

Her host consulted the menu. 'You've got time for a Macedonian Fruit Amphora,' said Eddie, flashing her a wolfish grin. 'The sound check isn't till four....'

Janice ripped the tape from the last carton of souvenir albums and peeked inside. Eddie, about to face a potentially problematical lunch date, carefully selected the quietest tie from the rack marked 'Forties Neckwear'.

'What d'you want me to do with the ones that don't have any grooves *or* holes in the middle, Mr Clockerty?'

Eddie knotted the scrambled egg-patterned tie round his neck and wrinkled his nose. What was that peculiar smell?

'D'you just want me to fling them in the bin with the rest of the rejects?'

Eddie sidled across the shop to where the MacAteer twins were out for the count in their go-chairs. He sniffed. 'Have you been feeding these toddlers drink, Miss Toner?'

Janice shoved the latest batch of sub-standard pressings into the large cardboard box destined for the back shop midden. 'I only gave them a drop in a cup. It was either that or stuff their nappies down their throats.'

She looked up, but Eddie was already out to lunch.

★

The only reason Suzi had agreed to turn up at the taverna was in the hope of seeing Danny, so what did the Majestics' manager mean, he couldn't face her?

'Neither young woman is pressing charges, you'll be glad to hear.' Eddie helped himself to some more stuffed vine leaves, confident in the knowledge that sooner or later the young woman could be coerced into replacing the indiscreet and embarrassing McGlone. By disassociating themselves from him, the Majestics might just be able to pull off a face-saving exercise when that bloody documentary went out. He ran his tongue under his top plate and looked across at Suzi who was still boggling at him in incomprehension.

'It was that Sunday we done the souvenir recordings....' Eddie tucked his napkin into his shirt collar and lowered

★

Bomba stood in the Manhattan Casuals doorway and looked up and down the street. Dennis was late.

'I just hope Vinnie appreciates what you're doin' for him.' Fud picked through the rack of jackets discreetly described on the torn piece of cardboard sellotaped to one of the jacket cuffs as 'Hollywood Cast-offs', checked the blurred name tag stitched into the one of his choice, and carried it across to the mirror.

'Shut your face, O'Donnell.' Bomba didn't turn round but kept an eye out for the Transit. Whatever he'd done hadn't been for Vinnie, it had been for the Majestics ... the bass player knew him better than that.

Fud slipped an arm into the sleeve and pulled the jacket round his shoulders. Paul Newman was obviously a lot more dinky than he looked on the big screen, he mused. The jacket was a bum freezer.

'Don't tell us you've fell for the burd? Is that how come you're happy for Eddie to give Danny Boy the heave-ho?'

'Shuttit, I said.' The drummer gave up the hunt for Dennis and came back inside the shop. 'And get that off, it looks totally stupit.'

Fud craned his neck to get a look at his new jacket from behind. 'No, I think I'll hang on to it. You'll notice it doesnae have a big yella streak down the back like some people's.'

There was a screech of tyres. Dennis's arrival was timely, his remark as he walked in less so. 'Dig the jacket, Francis.'

Bomba grabbed the roadie's jerkin. 'What the hell kept you? I've got these weans to get across to my mother's!'

One look from Dennis, and Bomba relinquished his grip on the faded denim. The roadie strolled over to the counter and had a peep behind to see if Janice was hiding there.

'I'll be outside in the wagon, you guys.' Fud swaggered gallusly to the door.

Dennis tried lifting the large cardboard box of albums that Janice had left on the counter while she went in search of bin bags. 'Sufferin' God....'

Bomba picked up one of the twins. 'You grab her....' He held the twin out to Dennis. 'I'll get the wee fulla.'

Dennis, already staggering out to the Transit with the box of what he'd failed to observe were reject souvenir albums, merely raised an eyebrow.

On being roused from their drunken slumbers, the twins raised Cain.

★

In the semi down the tree-lined avenue, Vincent's voice gave up the unequal struggle at the end of 'Only the Lonely' and he fell backwards into his chair. The rest carried on 'dum-dum-dummy-doo-wah-ing' till they all petered out.

Dennis took advantage of the lull to get to his feet. 'I better get off round the stores with these albums. Anybody want anythin' while I'm away? No? Good.' He negotiated Diver's outstretched legs and groped for the door handle.

Bomba returned from his reverie. 'We've got a sound check at four, don't forget.'

Dennis took a quick glance at Vincent's face. Sound checks were never easy. This one was going to be especially trying.

The front door slammed and everybody fell back into a torpor. Everybody except Diver, that is. He hadn't come out of his to fall back into.

The front door opened again. Who said life with a rock'n'roll band was unexciting, Danny observed morosely to himself.

The roadie's dumb features reappeared round the door. 'That's your manager just gettin' out of a taxi – thought I better warn you.'

Danny gave Diver's foot a prod. 'That's Eddie arrived to pass on his condolences, pal.'

Not a twitch nor a spasm.

'Er ... I think I'll go upstairs and feed the guppies, you guys.' MacAteer wandered across to the door and let himself out.

What guppies, thought Danny. He looked at Fud. Fud looked away.

At that moment Eddie came into the room, his arms outstretched. 'Vincent ... where's Vincent?'

Fud put a hand on Danny's shoulder. 'If I don't see you again,' he mumbled, 'all the best.'

But Danny wasn't listening – he was too busy catching Eddie's act.

'A young life – what can I say?'

That one caught Danny totally unprepared and he nearly choked. What turgid B movie had Clockerty got that line from?

Fud ducked under the manager's arms. 'I'll be upstairs with Bomba feedin' the guppies, all right?'

Diver, meanwhile, had pulled himself back into a semi-comatose state and was trying to get out of his armchair. He looked a complete and utter wreck. Eddie took a few faltering paces forward and clasped this broken husk to his bosom. 'Vincent, Vincent, Vincent....' He even produced a tear, no less, to back up this three-times evocation.

The pair of them crunched to and fro amongst the debris till at last Vincent managed to focus.

'Eddie? Lemme get you a drink.'

The legs went. Eddie caught him under the oxters and helped him back to his chair.

'Where is that dozy bitch? *Glenna?*'

Eddie looked at Danny as if it was all his fault, and then eased Diver down onto his air cushion with a 'Mind you don't sit on your crutch, old son.'

Vincent sat on his crutch and carried on bawling for the dead Glenna to bring everyone a drink.

Danny signalled to Eddie to take his hat off.

Then Vincent yelped as though he'd suddenly had a vision, drew his legs up and buried his face in his hands.

Danny pleaded with Eddie to say something, anything.

Eddie stood for a moment in thought, then the anguished look deserted his features. He bent over the harrowed guitar player and enquired gently, 'When did you get the guppies, Vincent?'

★

Suzi prised from the letter box the withered bunch of gardenias that Danny had had delivered, and let herself into the flat. She dumped her bags in the hall and walked the few steps to the living room door. She hesitated. Home Sweet Home. She pushed the door open. Sweet and Sour Home. She crossed to the fireplace and chucked the dead bouquet into the empty grate.

'What're you looking at?' Her reflection stared sullenly back at her from the mirror.

She picked up her guitar case and turned towards the door. What was she supposed to do, go back to waitressing?

She whipped round. 'I *am* doing the right thing. Shut-up!'

★

Dennis was beeling mad. He'd like to have seen Eddie's face if he'd been there when the guy in the first shop took those dud albums out of their sleeves.

Everybody hung on for dear life as the Transit took the corner. As they came out of the tailspin Bomba leaned forward behind Danny's back and whispered something to Eddie.

The roadie kept on ranting. 'I have to wait till I try offloadin' them before I find out they're faulty!'

What with him bawling and the drummer whispering, Danny was getting cheesed off. 'I don't know if your Maw ever mentioned it, MacAteer, but it's the height of bad manners to whisper into a manager's camelhair overcoat. If you've anythin' worth sayin' we'd all like to hear it ... right, Fuddo?' He turned to O'Donnell for support.

'I wouldnae bank on it, Danny Boy.'

Dennis, blissfully ignorant about most of what went on, took up the cudgels again. 'How much d'you want to bet it's somethin' to do with these duff records?'

But Danny wasn't so sure. He tried a spot of guesswork. They wanted him to elbow the Chubby Checker medley for tomorrow night, was that it? The handspring off the piano? No, no, hold on, he'd twigged ... the Gene Autry impression followed by the duckwalk, right?

When it came, it came totally out of left field.

'You're out, Danny Boy.' Fud looked grim as he delivered the bad tidings.

Dennis and Danny looked at each other. Eh?

'We had a meetin'.' Fud continued unhappily. 'I was outvoted two to one. Tell him, Bomba.'

But before Bomba could tell him anything the van had pulled up outside the Pavilion for the sound check.

'Fink! Scummy ratfink!' A furious Danny hared down the aisle and clambered onstage to reach Suzi who was standing at a mike tuning up.

'Who are *you* calling a ratfink, ya crummy two-timing....' Suzi shaded her eyes against the spotlight. 'Where are you?'

He was where he should be and she shouldn't, he fumed, onstage at the Pavilion for a Majestics' sound check.

'Get that stupid guitar off and get back home to your knittin'!' Who needed dolls coming along and spoiling everything?

Danny was determined to get that guitar off her if it was the last thing he ever ... *aaaaaaaaaaaaargh!* He'd reckoned without the drummer.

It wasn't so much Bomba's leaping onto his back from out of the blue, it was the fingers rammed up his nostrils that bugged him. He thought the drummer wasn't supposed to hold with chick singers?

'The boy McGlone's only standing in for the sick Vincent on this sound check, Dennis,' Eddie called out.

Danny made a mental note to gouge the manager's eyes out just as soon as he'd got his nose back.

'If it'd been anybody else but her I wouldn't've minded as much, ya dirty big midden!' screamed Suzi.

Anybody else but who? What was she talking about? Danny was confused. She wasn't referring to that embarrassing scene at the Holiday Inn when he'd had to beat Sheena Fisher off with a big stick, was she?

'I did stress it was all hearsay, Miss Kettles,' said Eddie hurriedly.

'You what?'

So, thought Danny, it was Edwardo that had snitched on them, was it?

'Ask yourself, Suzi,' Danny yelled through the pain, 'would I get up to something that gross just after you'd got a tankin' from that psychopathic dwarf of a husband of yours?' He felt a sudden searing stab of red-hot needles in his lower back, as if somebody had taken hold of the flesh and nipped it as hard as they possibly could.

'Don't you ever tell me to get back home to my knitting ever again, McGlone, d'you hear?'

★

The physical violence of the Pavilion had in some miraculous way served to loosen a few bricks in the wall which Suzi had built between herself and Danny, and he – ever the opportunist – had got a toehold in that wall and hauled himself over the top. His drop to the other side had been short and taken in the dark. Danny lay there in the blackness and thought about it. What did she mean, it was 'okay'? Three minutes was a whole heap better than lots of guys with shredded nerve ends and throbbing nostrils could manage. And anyway it was *five* minutes – he could see the luminous hands on the alarm clock from his side of the bed. He snapped on the reading lamp. 'It'll not always be a disaster!' He was out of practice on account of how he kept getting thwarted, right? *Right?*

'Is that you finished now?'

That was twice she'd said that in as many minutes. Danny wished she wouldn't, and said so.

'I mean, is that you finished going on about it?'

It wasn't *him* that was going on about it, Danny put her right, it was *her*. *He* thought it was wonderful. Considering it was their very first outing, it *was* wonderful. *Wasn't it?* He was positive he heard her sigh.

'It *was* wonderful, Danny.'

The sceptic in him said she was only saying that because he'd said it. 'Don't lie to me, Suzi.' He lay back and waited for her to rerun the entire three ... sorry, *five* minutes of carnal ecstasy in Panavision with Saul Bass titles.

'You want the truth, do you?'

Of course he wanted the truth. He switched out the light and stood by the imaginary projectors.

'All right ... it was okay.'

Right. That was it. Where were his underpants? He was leaving.

'My mind was on other things, that was all.'

Aw, yeah, that was precisely what a chap wanted to hear. Where the hell were his bloody underpants? 'Like what, for instance?' Danny felt under the bedclothes with his feet.

'Well, like tomorrow night....'

He hadn't done anything daft, like swallow them, had he?

'And beyond.'

Beyond? Danny brought his head up from under the sheets. After tomorrow night there was every chance there wouldn't be a 'beyond', he said with sarcasm. Certainly not for yours truly ... he'd been replaced – or had she forgotten about that already?

'Of course you haven't. Don't be stupid.'

It was okay for *her* to tell people not to be stupid. *She* was a Majestic – *he* wasn't.

'Vincent's never going to make the gig if what you lot told me's true....'

Aw, that was a great consolation, that was, Danny thought. First he had to step into the Big Bree's bootees, now he was supposed to step into Diver's! 'Thanks a bunch, Kettles.' If it hadn't been for his uncovered hurdies, he told himself, he'd've quit that bed there and then. As it was, he was so mad that he played his joker sooner than he'd intended. 'And while we're at it, how come you didnae trust me, eh?'

What'd he care it was a complete non sequitur? Ever since he'd stepped off that plane at Prestwick everything that'd happened to him had been a non sequitur, including this doll who was giving him a blank look like she didn't know what he was talking about. 'You don't imagine I spent all those evenings in that bathroom without makin' a complete inventory of your medicine chest, do you?'

That made her sit up.

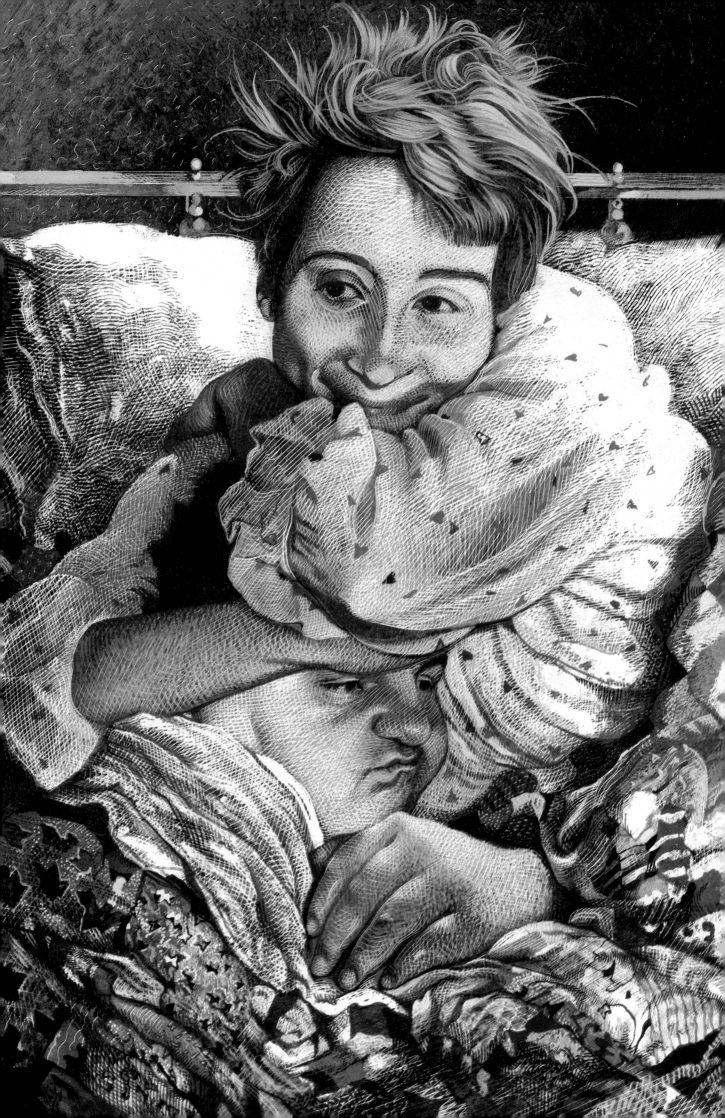

'I notice tonight some additional pharmaceutical para-phernalia....' He brought the home pregnancy testing kit from under the bed and kept it well out of her reach.

She went white.

'Don't worry, Suzi. Now that we've slept together....'

'*Forty winks*, McGlone!'

Danny was not to be thwarted. 'Now that we've slept together,' he repeated, 'I can in all conscience kid myself on it's mine when it arrives.' Yeah, he knew it was crazy and noble – but that was the kind of guy he was, right?

Kettles stared at him in utter disbelief.

'I know, I know. It's morally reprehensible, not to mention mildly medieval – but every wean's entitled to a Mammy *and* a Daddy in my book.'

Danny waited for her response. It was a long time coming.

'What is that – a psychiatric condition, a phobia, what? You're off your head, McGlone.'

That was true.

'I am perfectly capable of looking after my own child when it gets here.'

Which he also knew to be perfectly true. Except he was talking fiscally. 'You need dough to bring up a wean. What you goin' to do, go back to your old trade? I can see it now: "Desperate for a Drink? Come Inside and Be Served in a Hurry by One of Our Pregnant Bar Staff" ... aye, very good, Kettles.'

'I'm in a band, amn't I?'

Aye, for how long? 'You're only in there for Eddie Clockerty to have a go at scupperin' the TV show, stupid.' Instead of keeping his big mouth shut, to his horror Danny found himself going on.... 'You didnae think he was signin' you up on the strength of your good looks and talent, did you?' Mind you, he thought, Eddie Clockerty wouldn't recognise talent if you shoved Barbra Streisand down the front of your troosers and got her to sing 'Lullaby of Birdland'.

Suzi bristled. 'So what? I don't have to depend on the Majestics. There's about fifty paintings under this bed I can sell!'

There was what? Danny leaned over the side of the bed and hauled out something flat and square. God, talk about dark horses!

'Stop that!'

'They're not very good, are they? *Ow!*' That was another reason Danny wanted to find his underpants.

'Get your manky paws off! Who d'you think you are?'

'With any luck the future Mr Kettles – what d'you say, Suzi? I've got the perfect honeymoon spot all picked out.' He could wire the Funny Shoe Salesman, he thought, have him take a vacation, and they'd have the place to themselves ... and the cockroaches, of course. 'Bring your paintings. I'll touch them up for you....' Her response was deadly and he yelped in pain. Then the place was plunged into sudden darkness. It couldn't've been anything he'd said, could it? Desperately Danny tried to think how to worm his way back into her affections.... No, he'd already tried that one, with an actual scale model of a worm, and it had not been an out-and-out success. There had to be some other route.

'Er ... Suzi?'

'D'you want another skelp, McGlone?'

'No, a hot chocolate, I cannae sleep a wink.'

There was a longish pause.

'Me neither. You'll find the tin on the top shelf next to the crystallised figs.'

What was she asking *him* for? He didn't have any underpants on, he protested.

'Go on. Don't be lousy, Danny. I'm just getting my feet warm after that....'

'Yes, go ahead – say it ... that *fiasco*.' What was it with dolls, he thought in exasperation – they always had to rub it in. 'If the dentist was any better at it how come you left him, eh?'

He recognised the sigh.

'There are other things in life, McGlone.'

'Aw, so he *was* better at it?'

'I told you how bloody wonderful it was,' she snapped. 'What more d'you want? It was wonderful – the earth moved, the bed moved, the flowers on the wallpaper moved! Now get up and make us some hot chocolate, will you!'

Okay, okay, he'd only wanted to get at the truth.... He put his foot on the floor and stood on something slithery and peculiar.

'Er ... Suzi?'

'Yes, Danny ...?' She sounded worn out.

But not too worn out, he hoped, putting one leg into his slithery and peculiar underpants.

'After we've had our hot chocolate, d'you fancy ...?' Danny felt sure she could hear his heart pounding in the dark.

'Fancy what – a crystallised fig? No thanks, they're foosty.'

God, whatever happened to romance?

'This is your last chance. Are you getting in this car, Vincent Diver, or ...?'

Vincent banged his crutch on the passenger door. 'Beat it, Noreen.' If there was one thing he couldn't stomach it was an 'understanding' woman. 'I don't want to be understood, understand?'

'Right.' Noreen got back into the Morris Minor and slammed the door. She jammed her foot to the floor and the engine coughed politely.

Vincent rammed his crutches into a craze in the paving stones and swung himself round. His words were steeped in venom. 'Well, what d'you expect? I've went and lost the one thing in the world that you could never give us ... and before you come back at me with the funnies, no, I don't mean a fitted carpet, I mean a kid, right?'

His wife threw open the car door. 'She didnae do herself in because she *lost* a kid. She done herself in because she *found* one ... *you!*' Noreen stepped out onto the road.

'That's right, she even had me swallowing her fantasy for a while. . . .' She took a step forward and brought her eyes level with her husband's. 'Then I thought back and remembered your sperm count.'

The clatter of the crutches hitting the pavement rang the length of the tree-lined avenue. Vincent's knees sagged, then gave way altogether. His coccyx hit the edge of the kerb and sent a jarring pain juddering through his recently stitched loins.

Remembered his what?

'More fool me for letting you believe all these years that it was *my* fault we couldn't have any!' Noreen stepped back into the car and this time the engine roared into life.

★

Eddie rested his little pot of Greek yogurt on the edge of the royal box at the Pavilion Theatre and tried counting the house. It was early days yet. At least the dozen or so who were there already wouldn't get the chance to be put off by the TV, that was something. He took the little spoon from Janice and dipped it in. After waiting a fruitless three and a half hours at the Greek taverna for Sheena Fisher to turn up and discuss the wording of the proposed disclaimer, Eddie's appetite had gone. All he could manage was a little yogurt.

'No, no, I think it was a very caring thing to do,' Janice said. She'd known all along it was Eddie who had written to Noreen blowing the whistle on Vincent. He'd got her to post the letter. 'Shame about wee what-d'you-call-her, though. Still, I don't think there was much future in knittin' lumber jackets for the criminally insane. What d'you reckon, Mr Clockerty?'

But Eddie was too busy spilling yogurt down the front of his camelhair coat to come up with a coherent answer to that one.

Vincent stumbled, tried valiantly to press on, then ground to a halt outside a large electrical goods store but a scant quarter-mile from his destination. The Great March was almost over . . . all he needed was a short respite and a little refreshment. He released his arms from the elbow-rings in the crutches, rested the crutches against his left hip and reached into his back pocket for the half bottle of Smirnoff. He unscrewed the cap and put the bottle gratefully to his lips.

Behind him, in the store window, fifty-seven TV sets featuring fifty-seven images of his younger self silently mocked. The crippled guitarist, unaware of this battery of twenty-two-year-old electronically relayed Vincents at his back, lowered the vodka bottle and gulped down a lungful of evening air. He gave his chest a bang with the flat of his hand and swivelled from the hips to replace the almost empty bottle in his jeans pocket. A primal scream that started in his lower abdomen fought its way through his lights and liver and came gurgling up his windpipe. When he caught sight of his reflection superimposed on his multiplicity of younger selves the scream almost blew the teeth out of his gums. The vodka bottle leaped from his fingers and shattered on the pavement. His knees buckled and he went down, sending the crutches clattering into the gutter. . . .

Dennis perched himself between Eddie and Janice in the royal box and congratulated himself on his quick thinking. 'I got them to put the boy's name back up on the marquee.' He turned expectantly to Eddie.

Eddie shot Janice his blackest look. He might have dropped a line to Noreen giving Vincent away, but he was hardly likely to do so to the Customs and Excise giving *himself* away . . . stupid girl.

'I said, I got them to put the boy's name back up . . .,' repeated Dennis, only louder this time.

Janice leaned forward. 'You know who I think it was, Mr Clockerty? D'you remember that boy that came round to the shop after closin' time lookin' for a refund and you slipped a note under the door claimin' to be a registered blind person?' She was determined to run this particular hare to ground.

Dennis decided to have a last stab at letting Eddie know how he'd managed to save the big gig. 'Vincent hasnae showed up so I got them to put the boy's name back up . . . are you listenin'?'

Eddie broke off counting the house. 'What boy?'

Janice placed a hand on Dennis's thigh and brought her face close to Eddie's. She kept her voice low. 'The boy with the meat cleaver . . . the one that bought the Frankie Avalon loafers, remember?'

Dennis threw back his head and howled at the painted stars on the Pavilion roof.

The musty curtains parted behind them and Noreen stuck her head into the box. 'I've walked him around the block a few times. He'll be fine now.'

Eddie abandoned his census with bad grace. He turned to face Noreen. '*Who'll* be fine?'

As Vincent limped slowly out of the wings and into the light, the front two rows of the stalls got to their feet and gave the Majestics' veteran guitarist a standing ovation. Danny and Suzi, well into the second chorus of 'Tutti Frutti', upped the decibel level in an effort to top the rammy from the Diver fan club – but to little avail. Row upon row rose or half-rose to pay homage. Vincent acknowledged the audience's accolade with a cursory wave and strapped on his trusty Gretsch. A few choice licks and a couple of bum notes later he was well into the Little Richard favourite, bopping stiff-leggedly to the combined beat of the MacAteer and O'Donnell rhythm section.

Danny glanced across at Suzi, who was giving it laldy on her Veri-thin. It was certainly good to be back sharing a stage with her. Even sharing one with Diver wasn't all that terrible. He caught Vincent crabbing across to Fud and shouting something down the bass player's ear before leading the band into 'Almost Grown', the hardest-won single in the entire history of rock'n'roll. The Inverbervies and the Saxophone Brothers swung onstage in glorious augmentation. Suzi chucked a dazzling smile in Danny's direction. Danny felt as if his heart was going to pop out of his shirtfront and bop all over the stage. The audience roared.

'How're you feelin', Kettles?' yelled Danny above the soaring rhythm.

'Sick, Danny,' cried Suzi.

'I love you!' Danny bawled.

'That's why I'm feeling sick, dummy,' she shouted back.

They reached over and kissed.

The Majestics segued back into 'Tutti Frutti' with the Ceilidh Quintet and the Sax Bros in hot pursuit. It was a magnificent sound.

Out of the corner of his eye Danny saw Vincent douse himself and his Gretsch in some sort of clear liquid from a big flagon. Then, to his utter astonishment, he watched him flick at the stupid lighter he'd got off Glenna. What in God's name was the eejit playing at?

'A-wop boppa loo bop, a-wop bam....'

BOOM!